Reader Praise f
Melody Carlson's Diary of a Teenage Girl Series

"I absolutely love all of your books. I feel like you totally connect with all that goes on in my life, and I'm sure lots of other girls feel that way too. Thank you so much for these books. They changed my life."
—SHADWA

"Your books are awesome! They really touched and inspired me."
—CASSAMAR

"Melody, I love your books. I just finished the Caitlin series and have to say they were amazing."
—JANELLE

"I want to let you know that your books have had such an impact on my life."
—LEAH

"I love your books! They've really helped me to grow in God."
—MISSY

"Your books are so spiritual and awesome. All of your words in your book have helped me so much with becoming closer to God. You have set such an amazing example.... Thank you."
—MEGAN

PAPUA NEW GUINEA

notes from a spinning planet

a novel

Melody Carlson

WATERBROOK
PRESS

NOTES FROM A SPINNING PLANET—PAPUA NEW GUINEA
PUBLISHED BY WATERBROOK PRESS
12265 Oracle Boulevard, Suite 200
Colorado Springs, Colorado 80921
A division of Random House Inc.

The characters and events in this book are fictional, and any resemblance to actual persons or events is coincidental.

13-Digit ISBN: 978-1-4000-7145-6

Library of Congress Cataloging-in-Publication Data
Carlson, Melody.
    Notes from a spinning planet—Papua New Guinea / Melody Carlson. — 1st ed.
        p. cm.
    Summary: Traveling in Papua New Guinea with her journalist aunt, twenty-year-old Maddie becomes fast friends with Lydia, a young woman with dreams of becoming a medical doctor—and a very dark secret.
    ISBN-13: 978-1-4000-7145-6
    1. Papua New Guinea—Juvenile fiction. [1. Papua New Guinea—Fiction.
2. Aunts—Fiction. 3. AIDS (Disease)—Fiction. 4. Christian life—Fiction.
5. Voyages and travels—Fiction.] I. Title.
PZ7.C216637 Now 2007
[Fic]—dc22

                                            2006030332

Printed in the United States of America
2007—First Edition

10 9 8 7 6 5 4 3 2 1

ONE

*I*t's amazing how much more comfortable I feel on this trip. Nothing like when my aunt and I flew to Ireland a couple of months ago and I was a total basket case. Not that I'd exactly call myself a seasoned traveler. That would be a huge overstatement. But as I snooze and read and basically just chill on the first leg of my latest journey with Sid, flying high over the Pacific, I think maybe I've evolved just a little.

"Listen to this, Maddie," says Sid. My aunt's been poring over a bunch of articles that an editorial assistant downloaded onto her laptop just before we left. "Instead of protecting the public and children from violence, it is the police who are committing some of the most heinous acts of violence imaginable."

"Huh?" I look up from a Margaret Mead book I'm reading, one that Sid recommended called *Growing Up in New Guinea.* "What?"

"It's from an article about human rights atrocities being committed in Papua New Guinea." She frowns as she removes her reading glasses. "It's really tragic. I had no idea."

"Is that going to be the focus of your article?" Sid and I are headed to Papua New Guinea, or PNG, which is less of a mouthful, so she can find out how the country has changed since emerging from the Stone Age into the new millennium.

"I'm not totally sure. But I'd like to find out." She taps her computer screen. "And listen to this quote, Maddie. 'As a result of HIV/AIDS, Papua New Guinea could lose up to thirty-eight percent of its working population by the year 2020.'" She turns and stares at me. "Can you imagine how many people that would be?"

Actually, I can't. Numbers have never been my strong suit. Still, I know that thirty-eight percent is a lot, and I suppose 2020 isn't that far off, even if it sounds like another lifetime to me.

Then Sid spews some more statistics, telling me that although PNG is somewhat remote, its number of AIDS cases is far higher than any of its neighboring countries. She also explains how inadequate the country's health-care and medical facilities are, and I'm starting to feel seriously concerned. In fact, I'm beginning to wonder why I agreed to come with Sid on this trip in the first place.

Okay, it's not like I came along just for the fun of it. I mean, seeing a third-world country did sound exciting to me, but I realize we're on something of a mission too. A mission to find Sid's story—whatever it might be. Her boss, John Something-or-other, has a real soft spot for this country. Sid said he's been concerned about the changes the culture has gone through since he was last there eons ago. As a result he pulled out all the stops and sent her to uncover some big story. Sid writes for one of the largest magazines in the world. The problem is, she's not totally sure what that "big" story is going to be or if it's even big at all. "But it'll be an adventure," she assured me when she invited me to join her.

Now I don't want to become overly critical of the country I'm about to visit, but hearing these sad reports of corrupt police and what seems like a hopeless AIDS epidemic, well, it just doesn't make Papua New Guinea sound terribly inviting. And it doesn't sound much like Margaret Mead's version of a rustic yet peaceful South Pacific culture. Of course, she wrote the book I'm reading about a hundred years ago, but according to my aunt, Mead's observations are still a good historical reference. Even so, I'm having a hard time staying focused on her quaint little tales now. I have to wonder what caused this country to go from a bunch of happy tribal, island people to a crime-ridden country that sounds like it's in serious peril. And I'm actually feeling pretty depressed about this whole trip right now.

"Oh, Maddie," says Sid, studying my face closely. "I'm sorry to have gone on and on about these things."

"That's okay," I tell her, forcing a little smile.

"No." She firmly closes her laptop and shakes her head. "I shouldn't have put all that on your shoulders."

"But I need to know what we're getting into." I sigh. "Even if it is pretty sad. I mean the facts are the facts, right?"

"But I hadn't meant to talk about business just yet."

"Why not?"

"Oh, just because." Sid gets a hard-to-read look on her face.

"But I thought I came on this trip to help you," I remind her, feeling like I've already failed, like maybe she's regretting her choice to bring me along, like she thinks I'm too young to deal with this. "I need to be aware of what's going on."

"True."

I feel the need to reassure her of my ability to handle this. "I'll admit it's kind of depressing. But it makes me curious too. I mean how does a place like New Guinea become like that? Margaret Mead's book makes the country sound so untouched and remote, and the people seem to have this childlike innocence. Well, for the most part anyway. They also have some pretty strange ideas about a few things. But they seem very moral and proper, especially in regard to sex. Mead even calls them puritanical. What happened?"

"Things must've changed."

"Well, I'd like to figure it out. I'd like to know what made their country change."

"You're sounding more and more like a journalist, Maddie."

I smile at her and inwardly sigh with relief. "Thanks."

"Just the same, I really didn't want us to get buried in all this… not yet."

"Why not?" I ask again, curious as to her sudden change of attitude. "I thought that's what this trip was about."

"As I told you, Maddie, this trip is also supposed to be your birthday present. I don't want to see you all serious and gloomy on your birthday."

I laugh. "You mean the birthday that will never be?" I'm well aware that we'll be passing over the International Date Line during this trip. This will automatically kick me out of August 9, my twentieth birthday. As a result, August 9 will be erased from my life-experience calendar forever—the day that never was, at least for me. It's kind of weird but kind of cool.

"Hey, someday you might thank me for skipping that day," she points out. "Instead of being fifty in thirty years, you'll only be forty-nine."

"But I *want* to turn twenty! It sounds so much more sophisticated than nineteen. I mean, maybe I'll make that missing birthday thing work for me when I'm really old," I say for her benefit, "but for now I'm proclaiming myself to be twenty. Okay?"

"Not so fast, Maddie. You're not twenty yet."

"So you mean I have to wait until we actually cross the date line?" I glance at my watch, which is still on Pacific Daylight Time, and it says it's 1:36 p.m. "When will that be anyway? The middle of the night?"

She just laughs and reopens her laptop, but she also has this slightly mysterious expression on her face. Like maybe she's got a surprise up her sleeve. Perhaps a mini–birthday cake hidden back there with the flight attendants. Hopefully chocolate.

Anyway, I can't be too bummed about the skipped date since my family and friends already celebrated my "unbirthday" before I left. My best friend, Katie, who is thankfully no longer engaged, threw a very cool surprise party for me just yesterday. Of course, they all gave me a bad time about having my birthday "erased" by the International Date Line, teasing me that I'd still be nineteen when I came back. After a while, I almost started to wonder.

Consequently, I did a little research of my own last night. I was curious as to why the world even needs an International Date Line in the first place. But it seems that if a traveler went west all the way around the world, journaling the days or marking them off the calendar, that person would end up with one extra day by the time he got home. Now that seems a little crazy, but it's true. It has to do with clocks and time-zone changes and the globe spinning, and to be perfectly honest, it sort of messes with my mind a little.

Some of the passengers on this flight are pretty stoked because their final destination is Honolulu, Hawaii. The rest of us will remain on board this "direct flight" to Sydney, Australia. We're only stopping there so the plane can be refueled for the second leg of our journey. I already told Sid that I'd love to get off the plane just so I could brag to my friends that I'd been in Honolulu, even if only for a few minutes, but she said that would probably be impossible, due to security. Even so, I think I can still *say* I was in Honolulu, even if my feet never actually touched the ground. At least I've got a window seat on the left side of the plane, which, according to the flight attendant, should help me get a quick peek at Pearl Harbor right before we land and maybe even Diamond Head after we take off again. Then we'll fly all night and reach Sydney the morning of August 10. And August 9 will be permanently erased from my calendar. So weird.

After a while Margaret Mead puts me to sleep. When I wake up, I can hear the pilot announcing that we're only fifteen minutes from landing. I push up the vinyl window shade and look out in time to see amazingly blue water and some green and brown islands below. "It's so beautiful down there," I say longingly to Sid.

"Uh-huh." Her nose is still in her computer.

"The water is all these shades of blue," I tell her. "Sapphire, turquoise, aquamarine…and it's so clear I'm sure I can see the bottom of the ocean."

"Uh-huh," she mutters again. Whatever she's reading must be really interesting—probably depressing too.

I want to ask a flight attendant to point out Pearl Harbor, but they're already getting buckled into their jump seats, preparing for the landing. So I just look and try to figure things out for myself. Too bad I didn't think ahead to get a travel brochure or something. Well, if nothing else, I can say that what little I saw of Hawaii was really, truly beautiful. Maybe Papua New Guinea will be beautiful too.

It's 1:48 p.m. when we touch down in Honolulu—Hawaii time, that is, which I understand is two hours earlier than Pacific Daylight Time. Still, I don't readjust my watch yet. Why bother? I observe some of the other passengers standing up and cramming themselves into the narrow aisles as they pry pieces of luggage out of the overhead compartments. It's actually kind of funny. Like, what's the hurry? The doors aren't even open yet. But they eagerly stand there with their bags and purses and briefcases and things, just waiting. It reminds me of our cows back home when it's close to feeding time. They'll simply line up and wait and wait. Sometimes they'll wait a couple of hours. Finally the passengers begin slowly moving toward the exit. They still remind me of cows as they amble along. It's all I can do to keep from mooing as they go past. Or maybe it's just Hawaii envy. I really should grow up.

"You ready?" asks Sid suddenly. Then she closes her laptop and slips it into her briefcase.

"Ready for what?"

"To get off the plane."

"Really?" I say hopefully. "We can get off?"

"Yes," she says. "Didn't you hear the flight attendant say that we can get off here if we want while they clean up for the next flight?"

"No." I look around and notice that a lot of passengers are remaining in their seats. But maybe they've set foot in Honolulu before.

"I guess you were asleep," she says as we stand up. "The layover is at least two hours." She stands and reaches for her carry-on. "Oh yeah, if we get off, we're supposed to remove our carry-on items too. It's a security thing."

So we both get our carry-on pieces and exit the plane. I have to admit it feels so great to stretch my legs, and at least now I can honestly say that I've really been in Honolulu, even if it's only the airport. Katie will be impressed.

"Hey, do you think I have time to find some postcards?" I ask. "Or do we have to stick around here, close to the plane?"

"I think you have time," she says. "Let's walk this way."

So we walk for what seems quite a ways through the terminal, going past lots of gates, and the next thing I know we've gone right past the security check too. "Aunt Sid," I say, "we've gone too far! Now we'll have to go back through security."

She laughs. "Not today, we won't."

"Huh?"

"Happy birthday, Maddie!" She unzips her carry-on and pulls out a slightly rumpled paper lei, then puts it around my neck and gives me a big hug. "Aloha, sweetie, and welcome to Honolulu!"

"What?"

"We're staying in Honolulu, Maddie."

"What about Papua New Guinea?" I ask with concern. And,

okay, this seems pretty weird, because I was beginning to dread going to our final destination, but now I'm suddenly worried that this is it—that we're not going any farther than Honolulu! As much as I want to see Hawaii, I don't want to miss going to New Guinea.

"Oh, don't worry," she tells me. "This is just a little layover. A birthday surprise for you. I didn't really want you to miss your birthday as we flew over the International Date Line."

"Really?"

She nods. "Yes. We have two days to do whatever we please in Honolulu. And then it's back on the plane and off to the other side of the planet." She smiles at me. "So you really do want to go to Papua New Guinea after all?"

"Of course!"

We collect our checked bags and get into a hotel limousine, which takes us to a very cool hotel right along Waikiki.

"Swanky," I say as we go into a very luxurious room that overlooks the beach.

"Swankier than the inn in Clifden?" she teases.

I mentally compare this place to our ocean-view digs in Ireland. "You know, they're both swanky in their own way."

She nods. "I'm glad you can appreciate a variety of cultures."

"I'm learning."

She tosses her bags onto one of the queen-size beds and stretches her arms. "Ah, this is just the kind of break I need right now."

"Man, am I glad you told me to pack a swimsuit," I tell her as I look out the window to see tall palm trees and white sand and miles and miles of varying shades of bright aqua blue water.

"Ready to hit the beach?" she says.

"Woo-hoo!"

We change and gather our beach stuff, then make a quick exodus to the seaside, where I splash around in the energetic waves, which are surprisingly warm and nothing like the chilly Pacific in Washington State. I even let a couple of friendly guys give me some tips on body surfing, which is way harder than it looks. And finally, feeling totally relaxed and happy, I flop onto a towel next to my aunt and soak up the last rays of afternoon sun.

I could so get used to this!

TWO

*W*e rent a car for our second day, also my birthday, in order to tour Oahu, the island where Honolulu is located. I've learned that the major Hawaiian islands are Kauai, Oahu, Molokai, Lanai, Maui, and Hawaii (the biggest), but there are lots of other, smaller islands too. They're all part of a volcanic mountain chain, and if we had more time, Sid said we could take a helicopter tour of one of the active volcanoes and see some red-hot, bubbling lava.

But I'm cool with seeing the island via this light blue Sebring convertible. We've got the top down, and I wish I could drive, but, alas, even though I'm twenty, I'm still too young to drive a rental car.

"Want to do the typical tourist things today?" asks Sid as we drive out of Honolulu. We've already packed our swimsuits, towels, and snorkeling gear that we rented from a shop by the hotel.

"Since I've never been here before, it's all new to me," I tell her. "What would you recommend?"

"There are some things that are worth seeing, like Diamond Head, which isn't too far from here. And then there's Iolani Palace, which we might want to save for tomorrow since it's not far from the hotel and it'll be short day. There's the Polynesian Cultural Center and, of course, Pearl Harbor and the USS *Arizona* Memorial."

"It all sounds good to me," I tell her, leaning back in the seat and looking out at the view, which is so different from the Washington farmland I'm accustomed to seeing every day.

"Naturally, we'll fit in some snorkeling. I remember snorkeling on a reef on the West Shore, Makaha Beach Park, about ten years ago. As I recall, it was pretty nice. We could hit that in the afternoon."

"Are you sure I'll get the hang of snorkeling?"

"You're a good swimmer, Maddie. I don't see why it should be a problem. And we've got those vests to help keep us afloat. I think we'll be fine."

"What about sharks?"

She laughs. "I don't think we need to worry."

So we stop at Diamond Head, and the view from up here is really stunning. I still can't believe how crystal-clear the water is. The ocean reminds me of a giant jigsaw puzzle, but all in gorgeous shades of blue. I take some photos, but I'm not sure they'll show the true beauty. Then we stop at the Sea Life Park and check out the dolphins and other sea animals before we head up the East Shore toward the Polynesian Cultural Center, which is really pretty interesting even if it is kind of touristy. It's a good way to see what old Hawaii was like, to pick up some history and sample some traditional Hawaiian foods, which are incredibly yummy.

We drive on around the north side of the island, taking a nice break at Sunset Beach, where we watch some surfers doing their thing. We cool off in the water, then catch some sun and a little rest.

"So how are things with Ian?" I ask Sid as we relax on the beach. I've been dying to ask her this since yesterday but didn't want to appear overly eager. Ian McMahan was my aunt's "true love" when she was about my age. They parted ways back in the seventies but then met up again just a couple of months ago while we were visiting Ireland. I had a little something to do with it, so naturally I'm interested in hearing how it's going.

"We're staying in touch," she tells me as she turns over onto her stomach.

"Uh-huh?"

"We e-mail pretty regularly…"

"And?"

"And…we'll see…"

Okay, I'm thinking if I'm going to become a good journalist, I'll have to improve my investigative reporting skills. Still, there's time. I remind myself that Sid and I are spending two and a half weeks together.

"And how's Ryan?" my aunt asks as she rolls over and peers at me from beneath her oversize dark glasses.

I just shrug. "You should know," I say offhandedly. "You've practically adopted him as your surrogate son, haven't you?"

She laughs. "Of course. But how are things between you and Ryan from your perspective, Maddie? I got the distinct impression that you were interested in him just as we were leaving Ireland. Was there anything to that?"

I shrug again. "I don't know."

"He told me you guys have been e-mailing each other too."

"Yeah. He's been encouraging me to transfer to the University of Washington. For journalism."

She chuckles. "Sounds like a great idea to me."

"I figured you'd think so since it's your alma mater."

"It's a good school, Maddie. And, as I've said before, if you need to pinch pennies, you could stay with me in Seattle."

"Well, I've been seriously thinking about it, Sid."

"About ready to get off the farm?"

I sigh. "Yeah. Ever since we went to Ireland, I've been thinking it's time for me to step out and try something new."

"How do your parents feel about it? Wasn't the plan for you to move on after finishing your sophomore year?"

"Yeah, but I think they understand. Community college might be good for saving money, but the classes aren't all that challenging. I've already looked into transferring to the university for winter or spring semester."

"Cool."

"I heard it's easier to get in then since fall is when everyone else is trying to enroll."

"Makes sense."

After a little snooze, we pile our stuff back into the car and head on around to Makaha Beach Park, where I snorkel for the first time. Sid gives me some lessons, reminding me again and again to "just relax."

"Focus on breathing through your mouth and relaxing," she says. "And don't think about it too much, or you'll psych yourself out."

We go out a ways, and I do see a few fish, which are amazing, but the waves are pushing me around, and I manage to gulp down enough seawater to take the fun out of it.

"We'll have to find a calmer spot," she tells me after I fall down in the surf several times while trying to remove my flippers and extract myself from the waves. I'm glad no one has a camera, since I must look like a total dork. I'm sure I have about a pound of sand in my swimsuit too.

"It was actually kind of cool for a little while," I tell her, "but kind of overwhelming too."

"We'll go to Hanauma Bay tomorrow," she says. "It's close to Honolulu, and it's supposed to be spectacular. Plus there's not much wave action."

"Sounds good."

We drive on around the island, finally stopping at Pearl Harbor and going onto the USS *Arizona* Memorial, which is sort of eerie and fascinating, a ghostly white structure that hovers over the place where the USS *Arizona* was sunk. It's hard to believe that eleven hundred young men about my age were killed here—or that their bodies are entombed in the sunken ship, which was attacked by Japan during World War II. There are a couple dozen other people at the memorial, but I notice one elderly woman in particular. Her hair is snowy white, and she's hunched over. She uses her walker to slowly navigate her way to a place where she can stand by herself. There she removes a lei of purple orchids from around her neck, then drops it over the side. She leans over and watches as it tumbles down and lands in the water. I can't help but wonder if her sweetheart was lost here. Was it a husband, boyfriend, fiancé? Obviously it was someone dear to her. I can see it in her face.

Sid and I don't say anything as we leave the memorial. But I suspect she was just as touched as I was by the elderly lady.

"We better get a move on," she says as she starts the car.

"What's the hurry?" I ask.

"We have dinner plans," she says with a mysterious grin. "Remember, it is your birthday, Maddie."

"Oh yeah."

So we go back to the hotel, and after a shower and short nap, Sid tells me to put on something nice but comfortable. Then we head downstairs and outside to where the sun is just going down and tiki torches are being lit. Music is playing, and something smells delicious.

"It's a luau," Sid tells me, "for your birthday."

"They're having a luau for my birthday?" I say in astonishment.

She laughs. "Actually, they were already having a luau, but it was sold out. Then when I told them it was your birthday, they decided to make room for two more."

"Cool!"

The food is incredible. The fruit is awesome—I've never tasted things like papaya or mango, but I totally love them. And the pineapple is amazing. But it's the *kalua pua'a* that really knocks my socks off. Basically it's pork that's cooked in a pit with seasonings, and it's fantastic. I wish my dad, the barbecue king, could learn to do pork like this. But there's more going on than just food. The music is great, and the fire dancing is spectacular, although this old dude at our table, who seems to know everything, explains that the whole fire thing isn't an authentic Hawaiian tradition but something they only do for tourists. Whatever. I think it's cool. Then I'm invited up to the front for hula lessons, which I'm not half bad at, and I'm only slightly embarrassed when everyone sings "Happy Birthday" to me.

"Isn't this a little better than losing August 9 as we cross the International Date Line?" Sid asks as they bring the dessert.

"Thanks so much," I tell her. "This is a birthday I'll never forget!"

The next morning we get up early to go snorkeling at Hanauma Bay, which is totally awesome. It's like swimming in a giant saltwater aquarium. Without the wave action knocking me around, I get the hang of snorkeling fairly easily this time. I never knew there were so many different kinds of fish (they say there are more than four hundred species here!), and we even follow a great big green sea turtle for a while. Very cool.

Okay, there is one gloomy part of this day, at least for me, but I don't mention it to Sid. There's this guy hanging by the bathrooms who is obviously homeless and not well. He has on more clothing than a person needs on a warm day like this and open sores on his face, but what really gets me is the empty expression in his eyes. He looks totally hopeless. Sid manages to ignore him as she walks past, but I can't bear it. While I'm in the bathroom, I get a ten-dollar bill out of my purse and then, while Sid's still washing her hands, I slip out and give it to the man. He thanks me several times, and I say, "God bless you." It is such a small gesture, and I don't know how ten bucks will help him much, except maybe to buy him a couple of cheap meals at McDonald's. I wonder what his story is. Maybe it's drugs or maybe something more. But I do know this: God loves that man, and even if he uses the money for the wrong thing, it wasn't wrong for me to give it to him. I think he just needed to see that someone cared, someone noticed him, he wasn't invisible. I feel my eyes tearing up as I walk to the car.

I pray for the homeless man as we drive to Iolani Palace, the only royal residence in the United States. Of course, no royalty has lived there since the island monarchy was overthrown, long before Hawaii joined the States, but you can see that this amazing home was filled with every modern comfort way ahead of its time. I think about the king and queen who once lived here and the wealthy-looking tourists who are visiting the beautiful palace today. What a contrast between them and the man back at the bathrooms. It's hard to grasp the whole haves-and-have-nots thing. But it makes me sad.

All too soon it's time to say aloha to Oahu, and we head to the airport for our two fifteen flight.

"That was so great," I tell her after we make our way through security. "The best birthday present ever. Thanks, Sid."

"Good. I was ready for a little R and R myself."

Then I slap my forehead. "But I totally forgot to send postcards."

"It's not too late." She points to a newsstand with a large selection of Hawaiian postcards, and I pick out several and buy stamps as well. Before we board our flight, I drop my quick notes into a mailbox.

"Did you send one to Ryan?" Sid asks after we're seated in the plane.

I give her a smirky little smile. "Yeah. Just so happens I did." Then I nod to her laptop, which she was using at the airport. "Did you e-mail Ian?"

She gives me the same smirky smile back. And despite the fact that she's like thirty years older than me, I think we're a lot alike.

"Next stop: Sydney, Australia," says my aunt. Then she takes out a prescription bottle. "We don't want to forget our Malarone."

"Is that the malaria medicine?"

She nods. "We'll wait until they bring us dinner. It's best to take it with food."

"How long do we take it?"

"Two days before we get to New Guinea, which means we start today, and then every day we're there and for a whole week once we're back in the States."

"And that's it?"

"That's it."

So we take our Malarone with our evening meal, and the flight is, thankfully, uneventful. But the weird part is that, despite losing one whole day (August 11) when we crossed the International Date Line, and despite the fact that this is considered an overnight flight and we all pull the shades down and try to sleep, the sun never goes down. It's like the plane is chasing it around the world. So when we land in Sydney, it's eight in the morning, and there's the sun, still shining bigger than life. Bright and happy and ready for the "new" day.

"Man, this has gotta be the longest day ever," I tell Sid as we leave the plane.

"And it's only going to get longer," she points out.

The plan is to spend one night in Sydney. Originally that was simply a convenient travel arrangement. But while we were in Hawaii, Sid had her assistant set up an appointment with someone. I know she's trying to figure out the direction her article will take. Like she says, it's one of those "flying by the seat of one's pants" articles. And I'm getting the impression that if John, her editor, weren't so emotionally attached to the country, she wouldn't have taken this assignment at all. Still, I think it's exciting, and the idea of being in an exotic place like Papua New Guinea is fascinating. I can't wait to see what's ahead.

"I'm meeting with the local director of USAID today," she tells me as we stand on the airport sidewalk waiting for a taxi.

"What exactly is that?"

"It's an agency that works with developing countries like Papua New Guinea," she says as she waves down a cab. "The director will fill me in on what's being done to slow down the AIDS epidemic there. Right now that seems to be the biggest story in that country. You're welcome to come along if you like. I have a feeling it'll be mostly facts and figures and probably a little on the boring side. So I'll understand if you want to skip it. Besides, I'm sure you're worn out from the flight."

"I didn't sleep too well," I admit.

"Well, let's get checked into the hotel first," she says as we climb into the cab. "It's downtown and supposed to be very swanky."

I laugh, and the taxi driver says something to us, but I can't understand a word of it. I look at Sid, curious as to whether she can interpret this language, which I'm guessing is English, but his Aussie accent is so thick that it could be Swahili.

"The Radisson Plaza Hotel," she says to him.

He says something back to her, and I still don't get it. But she seems to be doing just fine. "Downtown," she tells him. And then he begins to drive.

"How can you understand him?" I say quietly.

"Yanks, are ya?" says the driver.

"Yes," says Sid. "We're Americans."

Then he says something that must mean "Where are you going?" And she says, "Papua New Guinea."

He makes a sour face. "Why d'ya wanna go thar?"

Okay, I got that.

She gives a quick explanation, and he makes some other comments that I can't completely get. But I can tell by his expression that he thinks we're crazy. Oh well.

After a while we're in the thick of downtown traffic, and finally he delivers us to a huge building, which Sid says is the Radisson. She pays him, and we get out.

"This hotel used to be an important Australian company," she informs me. "It's built like the Flatiron Building in New York. But now it's a hotel and a very nice one at that."

I have to agree with her when we enter the lobby. "This really *is* swanky," I tell her as we walk over to the concierge's desk.

We get checked in and take showers, and then it's time for Sid to go to her appointment at the USAID place. "Here's a walking map," she tells me. "There's a lot to see right near the hotel."

"Have you stayed here before?" I ask.

"Sure, a couple of times. They have a great pool and spa, if you're interested. I should be back around two." She sighs. "And then I might have to crash for a while myself."

I go back down with her, and then we part ways. She heads out in a taxi, and I, with walking map in hand, strike out to see a bit of Sydney. To stretch my legs a little, I head out to the Sydney Opera House for starters. I've seen photos of it, but it's even better up close.

It took seventeen years to build, but those huge white arches that resemble enormous seashells are well worth seeing in person. Then I walk through the Royal Botanic Gardens and past some historical buildings, although I'm not sure which is what, until I end up in a waterfront district called Woolloomooloo—I'm not making this up. Actually this area is very picturesque and has lots of unique little shops and galleries that I'm sure a person could spend days exploring. But I'm hungry, so I find a café and stop for some lunch.

Eventually my feet start moving more slowly, and I'm feeling exhausted. I head up Art Gallery Road, which leads past some more famous sites on the way back, but I'm too tired to care. Fortunately, my walking map finally takes me back to the hotel, where I go up to our room and instantly sack out.

Sid must've sneaked in while I was sleeping, and we both wake up around four in the afternoon. I'm wondering what time it is back in Washington. The chickens probably aren't even awake. But then I tell myself to just forget about it. There's no sense bothering yourself over time changes when you're away from home.

"I think I'll check out that pool," I tell Sid. "Maybe it'll help wake me up."

"I might join you," she says, "after I do some more research and write some notes before I forget."

"Was it a good meeting?"

She sighs. "I'm not sure. When it comes to the subject of the AIDS epidemic in Papua New Guinea, people seem to just throw up their hands and shake their heads like it's hopeless. It makes me wonder why John sent me over here. Well, except that he has such compassion for New Guinea. Did I mention that he spent a couple of years there with the Peace Corps during the sixties?"

"I'm surprised he didn't want to come himself."

She makes a face. "I think he knew it was going to be a great big bummer."

"Well, maybe we'll be able to figure things out better once we get over there," I say to reassure her.

"I hope so. At least I have some connections when we get to Port Moresby. The woman I met with recommended a certain AIDS clinic that's supposedly making progress." She sort of laughs. "Although the way the woman said it, I can't be too sure what she meant. I hope we're not going on a fool's errand, Maddie." She flops into a chair and lets out a dejected sigh.

I feel a sense of heaviness as I go down to the pool. I can tell that Sid's discouraged, and suddenly I'm beginning to wonder just why we are going to Papua New Guinea. I mean, if the place is so hopeless that the experts are throwing up their hands and shaking their heads, well, what difference will it make whether Sid writes a great story or not? And that makes me wonder what difference it will make that I'm here with her. I hope she doesn't regret bringing me along now.

And so as I swim some laps in the pool, I start praying. With each stroke, I ask God to do something miraculous for both of us in Papua New Guinea. I ask him to use me in a special way for Sid's sake. Maybe I'm just here to encourage her, or perhaps I really can help with her research. Or maybe I'll just carry her bags if she gets tired or even wash her feet if she needs it. I just want to do what I can to help her, and I pray that God will help me.

THREE

I borrow Sid's computer to check my e-mail the next morning. To my dismay there is nothing from Ryan. In fact, I haven't received anything from him since we left home. I've only e-mailed him once these past few days—a sign of self-control since I don't like to come across as overly eager when it comes to guys—and I repress the urge to e-mail him again now. Still, it worries me a little that he hasn't written. And it bugs me that it worries me. But I won't mention this to Sid.

We fly out of Sydney at eight thirty a.m. Even though the city was interesting, I'm relieved to go. It was just too big and busy for this country girl. We stop in Brisbane, Australia, and board a smaller plane that's owned by an airline called Air Niugini. I suddenly get the feeling that I'm really traveling to a very foreign country now. In fact, I start to wonder just how well-maintained this funky plane might be. It's some kind of turboprop, and it seems really ancient to me. Like something from an aeronautical museum. Just when I think I'm over my flying phobia! I mean, what if this plane's engines are really, really old? And do they even have certified mechanics in a backward place like Papua New Guinea? Sid hands me a travelers' booklet with some general information on PNG, which might be a good distraction.

"Just to bring you up to speed," she says loud enough to be heard over the noisy engines, "I mean, since Margaret Mead. I think a few things have changed."

I study the photo on the front of the booklet. It's of a man wearing a colorful feather headdress. His face is painted bright yellow and blue, and what looks like a bone or maybe some sort of animal tusk is pierced right through the center of his nose. "Doesn't look like fashions have changed too much," I say to her.

"Well, that's probably his ceremonial costume. Not an everyday sort of look. John said they have some amazing celebrations in the highland regions. The gatherings are called sing-sings, and the tribes dress up and compete against each other doing dances and things."

"Sounds interesting."

As I read, I learn that because of Papua New Guinea's location, just a few degrees from the equator, the climate is very tropical. Probably even warmer than Hawaii, which is not nearly as close to the equator. They also get a lot of rain. It seems that outsiders (Europeans) first arrived in this area in the sixteenth century, and it was later settled in the nineteenth century by the Germans and British. It was more recently governed by Australia until it gained full independence in 1975. Okay, enough for history. The pamphlet moves on to geography now.

It seems the island has quite a mountain range. The highest peak is nearly fifteen thousand feet, which is even taller than Mount Rainier! The eastern half of the island is Papua New Guinea, and the western half is a totally different country called Irian Jaya (Indonesia). It also sounds like most of the roads aren't very well maintained and most commercial transportation is by air or sea, which makes me wonder about my aunt's idea to get a rental car. *Note to self: ask Sid about this when we land.*

One of the most surprising facts is that there are over seven hundred different languages spoken among the various native tribes! And the country's population is only about five million, which is less than in Seattle's metro area. I try to imagine seven hundred different languages being used in the Seattle area. Kind of mind blowing.

"Okay, Maddie," says my aunt as she hands me her laptop, "I don't want to scare you, but I think you should be aware of a few things before we land. My assistant e-mailed me a statement from the U.S. Department of State, the Bureau of Consular Affairs, entitled 'Travel Warnings for Papua New Guinea.' I wish John had warned me about this."

"What?" I ask.

"See for yourself."

I brace myself as I begin to read the computer screen. Sid's face looks dead serious, and I'm wondering if she's having second thoughts about this trip. This is pretty disappointing since I've really been praying about everything, and despite the challenges I'm jazzed about what lies ahead. Like we're going to have this amazing adventure. No way do I want her to get cold feet and turn us back before we even get started.

She points to a section on the computer screen. "Read this."

CRIME: Papua New Guinea has a high crime rate. Numerous U.S. citizen residents and visitors have been victims of violent crime in recent years, and they have sometimes suffered severe injuries. Carjackings, armed robberies, and stoning of vehicles are problems in Port Moresby, Lae, and Mount Hagen. Pickpockets and bag-snatchers frequent crowded public areas. Hiking in rural areas and visiting isolated public sites such as parks, golf courses, beaches, or cemeteries can be dangerous. Individuals traveling alone are at greater risk for robbery or gang rape than are those who are part of an organized tour or under escort. Visitors to Papua New Guinea should avoid using taxis or buses, known as Public Motor Vehicles (PMVs), and should instead rely on their sponsor or hotel to arrange for taxi service or a rental car.

Road travel outside of major towns can be hazardous because criminals set up roadblocks near bridges, curves in the road, or other features that restrict vehicle speed and mobility. Visitors should consult with the U.S. Embassy or with local law enforcement officials concerning security conditions before driving between towns. Travel to isolated places in Papua New Guinea is possible primarily by small passenger aircraft; there are many small airstrips throughout the country. Security measures at these airports are rare. Organized tours booked through travel agencies remain the safest means to visit attractions in Papua New Guinea.

Feeling a little uneasy, I look back at Sid. "What does this really mean?"

"It means that New Guinea is a dangerous place. More dangerous than I realized. And now I'm feeling guilty that I didn't find out about this before bringing you here, Maddie. Your parents will kill me if anything happens to you."

I sort of laugh. "Nothing's going to happen, Sid."

"Well, I just want you to be warned. We really need to be careful. Okay?"

"Yeah…and I read something about the roads not being too well maintained," I tell her. "And then that bit about carjacking… Uh, do you still plan to rent a car?"

She frowns. "I'm not sure what I plan to do now. Well, besides giving John a big piece of my mind after we land—even if it is the middle of the night for him. He never should've encouraged me to invite you on this trip."

"We'll be okay," I assure her. "And you should be glad that you brought me along. It sounds like you'd be even less safe if you were traveling alone."

"Maybe…"

"And, really, I'm not scared," I assure her. Although I do feel a little concerned. I mean, that was an official government warning we just read. And the part about gang rape is particularly disturbing. For some reason I had assumed that New Guinea would be a lot like Hawaii, as in fun and interesting but certainly not dangerous. Now I realize this may not be the case. I'd like to ask Sid some more questions, but she already seems fairly upset. "Are you worried?" I finally ask.

"To be honest, I am, Maddie. John assured me this would be a 'great adventure,' but I left most of the basic online research to my assistant, and I'm not impressed with what I'm learning now."

"You mean because I'm with you?"

She sighs. "I *do* feel responsible for you, Maddie. Maybe the responsible thing would be for me to change your ticket and send you home as soon as we land."

"No," I protest. "Please, don't even think about that, Sid. I want to do this. And, really, I'm not afraid. I think John's right—it will be a great adventure."

She doesn't look convinced, but at least she smiles now. "Well, maybe we won't be totally on our own in the country. Yesterday the USAID director gave me the number for a certain Dr. Larson in Port Moresby. She recommended we contact him right away. She said he's lived there for years and will be glad to help us. I'll call him as soon as we land." She glances around the plane, almost as if she's worried someone in here could be dangerous. I look around too, but the passengers seem perfectly harmless to me. They mostly look like businessmen, some Asian, some white, and some dark-skinned people who I assume are from Papua New Guinea. I also spy a young mother with two preschool-age girls who are so cute. I don't think there's anything to be concerned about here.

"Maybe they sensationalize those travel warnings," I finally say, "just to keep the wimpy travelers out."

She chuckles. "Meaning we're not wimps?"

I nod. "That's right."

"Well, the USAID director gave me a couple of money belts to keep our passports and valuables in." Sid pulls out her briefcase and fishes out a white item that sort of resembles a belt with a zipper pocket and hands it to me. "I only took them to be polite, but now

I'm thinking maybe we should use them when we get into New Guinea."

"Okay." I wrap the white band around my midsection and adjust the Velcro closure in front.

Sid laughs. "You're supposed to wear it *beneath* your clothes."

"Oh yeah, right." I discreetly make the proper adjustments, and soon we've placed our passports and other valuables safely beneath our clothes.

We land in Port Moresby just a little past noon. Sid still seems fairly agitated, and I try to maintain a calm exterior for her sake. But the truth is I'm starting to feel nervous too. I mean, sure, I can act all nonchalant, but I'm the novice traveler here. Sid's been everywhere, and she's seen all kinds of things. If this is bothering her…well, maybe I should be afraid too. Or maybe it's just the added concern that I'm here with her.

The openness of the airport reminds me of the one in Honolulu, only it's much smaller and appears to be not quite as efficient. There are slow-moving fans overhead, and people don't seem to be in any big hurry to get their bags as they meander down the short terminal. Of course, we soon discover why that is.

After waiting nearly an hour for our bags, Sid is getting antsy. "What could possibly take this long?" she asks. "This is a *tiny* airport."

"It's typical," says an Asian man who's been chain-smoking since we landed. "Island time."

She nods. "Oh, well then."

"Sid," I begin carefully, "if I'm the reason you're feeling so worried, I wish you'd just relax. I totally trust your judgment. I mean, you've traveled so much. You've been in Iraq and Afghanistan, and I'm sure New Guinea is nothing compared to those places."

She forces a little smile. "Yes, you're right. Still, I can't help but feel protective of my only niece. And, trust me, I would've *never* taken you to places like Iraq or Afghanistan. But I honestly thought this trip was relatively safe."

"And it probably will be."

"Probably." Still, she doesn't look convinced.

"And you already left a message with the doctor," I remind her. "So maybe we'll be hearing from him soon."

"I hope so."

"Want me to see if I can go find us something to drink?" I offer. I'm hot and thirsty, and the smell in here is starting to get to me. I'm not sure how to describe it except to say that it's sort of like dirty socks mixed with rotting fruit.

"No." She firmly shakes her head. "Like I already said, I don't want you out of my sight just yet. And I don't want us to leave the baggage claim without picking up our bags."

So we stand there and wait for another ten minutes. Finally a sloppy pile of luggage is rolled out on a big metal bin, and everyone rushes over at once, and it feels like a clumsy circus as we try to find our bags.

"I think someone has tampered with my bag," Sid says in a quiet tone.

"How do you know?"

"I have a little trick." She glances over her shoulder. "I tie a piece of thread around the zipper pulls. If it's broken, well, you never know."

I frown at her bag. "Is there anything valuable in it?"

"No, of course not." She grins. "A seasoned traveler knows better than to check anything of value. That's why we have carry-on bags."

"So can we get something to drink now?" I am so thirsty. I feel like I've been in the desert for days.

"Yes. First we'll exchange some money. You want to do that while I call for the hotel shuttle service?"

"Sure."

She hands me a twenty. "Their dollars are called kinas, but I'm not sure what the exchange rate is." Then she stands by our bags, making her phone call while keeping her eyes on me as I head over to the exchange counter.

"United States dollars?" asks the man.

"I want kinas."

He nods. "For United States dollars?"

"Yes." Okay, I'm thinking that's obvious since I'm holding the bill in front of him, but whatever.

He pushes some buttons on a calculator, then takes my twenty and gives me back five bills with "10 Kina" on them and one that says "5 Kina," along with some coins. Now I'm not really sure if this is right or not, but he also gives me a handwritten receipt that says "K57.75," so I assume he knows what he's doing. Besides, it looks like a lot more than I gave him. Even so, I thank him.

He smiles and thanks me back as I gather up my kinas and go back to Sid, who is just finishing her phone call.

Then we go to a kiosk and buy two bottles of water, which cost ten kinas and aren't even refrigerated, but I'm so thirsty I don't really care. We lug our bags outside, where it's even hotter, and wait for the hotel shuttle. As we're standing out there, an unmarked car pulls up, claiming to be a taxi. The driver smiles and offers us a ride, and my aunt uses a polite but firm voice to refuse.

"You will wait a long time," he says temptingly.

"We'll be fine," she says back, waving the car away.

"Do you think he was a criminal?"

She shrugs. "Hard to say. But we're not taking chances."

Finally a beat-up station wagon with a Port Moresby Travelodge sign painted on the side pulls up. The driver hops out with a big smile. He looks like he's not much older than I am.

"I think this is our ride," says Sid, but I can tell she's still feeling uncertain.

"Where is the Travelodge located?" she asks the driver. I know she already has the address of our hotel, but I suspect this is her way of checking him out. Pretty smart.

"City center," he says with an accent. Then he pulls a slightly worn business card from his shirt pocket. "Here is hotel phone number. Are you Missis Chase?"

She smiles at him, and I think he just passed her test. "Yes."

So he loads our bags and opens the back door for us to get in. I feel myself sighing with relief as I sit down. Okay, this is probably the oldest and smelliest cab I've ever been in, but at least it seems to be legit. We leave the windows rolled down as he begins to drive, but the air is so warm and humid that it doesn't do much good in cooling things off.

One of the first things I noticed about Port Moresby, shortly after getting off the plane, was the smell. I wouldn't want to admit this, especially to anyone who lives here, but the smell reminds me of something rotten. It's sort of sweet, but not a good sweet, and at the same time it's sort of stinky. And the air is so thick with moisture, I'm surprised I can't actually see it. Still, I tell myself, I should be able to get used to this. After all, I grew up cleaning out horse and cow stalls. It's not like I'm not used to foul smells.

"Are you here for business?" asks our driver.

"Yes," says Sid.

"Oh, good." He nods.

"We're journalists," she continues. "We write for a magazine."

"You write?" he says with interest. "That's good."

I smile to myself. It's nice that Sid's including me in this. I do plan to help her with research and writing, but I wonder if the taxi driver really believes that I could work for a big magazine like she does.

As he gets into city traffic, Sid's cell phone rings. Her side of the conversation leads me to believe it's Dr. Larson, and I feel a small wave of relief.

"We're just on our way to the hotel now," she tells him. "As soon as we drop off our things, we'll come over to the clinic for a tour. Yes. Thank you so much. See you then."

We pull up in front of a hotel, and the driver carries our bags into the lobby for us. Sid gives him a tip, and he responds with a bright smile, which seems more directed at me than her. She appears to notice this too and gives him a quick scowl, which I assume is some kind of a silent warning. He backs off so quickly that I feel sorry for him. But when I see Sid's worried face, I feel even worse for her. Why can't she just chill?

"Sorry," she tells me, "but we've just got to be really, really careful."

I nod. "Yeah, I know."

She checks us in, and we go up to a fifth-floor room that overlooks the city and the bay. It's actually a pretty nice view.

"Well, this is encouraging," she admits as she looks around the neat room. "I think I was starting to expect the worst of everything." She points to the small television. "Who knew?"

"This is going to be okay," I tell her. "I've been praying about everything, and I really feel like God is with us, Sid."

She nods. "I hope so."

We change into cooler clothes, then head back downstairs for a late lunch. Just before three, Sid asks the concierge to call a taxi for us. This time the car that pulls up is clearly marked as a taxi, which is reassuring.

"Saint Luke's Clinic," says Sid. The driver turns and glances curiously at her, then begins to drive.

The clinic is less than a mile away. I'm thinking we probably could've walked, but I suspect Sid wouldn't be comfortable doing that. Maybe I wouldn't either.

"Have you figured out the focus of your story yet?" I ask as we ride.

"That's what I'm working on. Other than the Stone Age meets the new millennium angle, John was pretty vague about this assignment. I guess I should be flattered that he trusts me so much. But I'm starting to wonder if this was simply his attempt to get someone on the inside to uncover what's really going on here. I suspect he's heard some things that concern him, and he wants to find out if they are really true."

"Like the crime rate and the AIDS epidemic?"

She nods. "That's probably the direction I'll take with the article. But I want to be open; maybe there's another angle. And somehow we need to really work the human interest element into this."

I consider this, realizing that traveling with Sid as she researches her story is probably some of the best education I can get for a career in journalism. I really should be thankful—and I am.

We enter the low, white building and are met by a nice-looking young woman named Lydia Obuti. Introductions are made, and she informs us that she's a volunteer at the clinic. "Dr. Larson asked me to show you around," she says in perfect English. She hardly has an accent. "He'll meet with you at four fifteen."

"Thank you," says my aunt. "Are there many volunteers here at the clinic?"

"Funding is limited," she tells us as she leads us down the hallway, "so I come over and help out when I can."

"Do you work somewhere else too?" asks Sid.

She nods. "Yes. I work in a government office just a few blocks from here."

"It's nice that you take time to volunteer here," I say.

She smiles shyly, then nods. "Would you like the tour now?"

"That sounds perfect," says Sid.

So Lydia takes us around the U-shaped building, stopping here and there along the way to help patients who are in need. She refills water pitchers, helps a woman to the bathroom—simple things like that. But as she does these "little" things, I can see true kindness in her expression. I wonder if I would have it in me to do what she's doing. I see the open sores on the patients' hands and faces, the sad and empty looks in their eyes. Although I feel extremely sorry for them, I'm not sure I could pick up a tissue like she is doing just now and wipe a runny nose with such gentleness.

"*Apinun,* Adibi," she says to a woman who is sitting in the hallway.

"What does that mean?" I ask.

"It's pidgin English or, as scholars say, Neo-Melanesian, and *apinun* is a greeting. Like *afternoon*. Adibi is the woman's name."

"Apinun, Adibi." I try it out, and the woman actually smiles up at me and says, "Apinun," to me. She looks as if she enjoyed hearing her name spoken for the second time.

"Yes," says Lydia. "That's right." And so I try the greeting out on other patients, and they seem to enjoy this tiny bit of attention as well.

To me this clinic is like a miniature hospital. I think there are only thirty patient rooms total. Everything here seems pretty old-fashioned, almost as if I've stepped onto an old movie set. I don't see much equipment or the kinds of technical tools you expect to find in a regular hospital. Not that I've been in that many hospitals, but I do watch some of the medical shows on television occasionally. And, let me say, this one looks nothing like those. If anything, this place seems pretty stripped down and basic. I also notice that all the rooms and wards appear to be full. I haven't seen even one empty bed. In fact, some of the rooms seem overly full, so it's no wonder that the air in here is stuffy and stale. On top of everything, it's hot. There apparently is no air conditioning, and although the shuttered windows are open and the overhead paddle fans are running, the air feels stagnant to me. And it's starting to get to me.

Okay, I have to confess that I know enough about AIDS to realize it's not an airborne disease, but just breathing this hospital air is making me feel sicker by the minute. Maybe it's the heat or the humidity or the smell of a different country, or maybe it's just me—although I'm a farm girl, and I've smelled just about everything—but it's like I can physically smell the germs in the air. By the time the tour ends and Lydia takes us out into the courtyard to wait for Dr. Larson, I'm about to throw up. I sit down on a cement bench and hang my head between my knees, taking in slow, deep breaths to steady myself.

"Are you okay?" asks Lydia, placing a gentle hand on my shoulder.

"Sorry," I say, looking up at her and feeling ashamed. "I just got lightheaded or something."

"It's not easy to see these things," she tells me.

Sid nods sadly. "And from what I've heard, this is one of the best AIDS clinics in the country."

"We know it's not perfect. But we're proud of it. We do our best."

"Everything seemed very clean in there," I say in what I hope is an optimistic tone. I really don't want to offend Lydia. She's such a sweet and caring person.

She smiles at me. "Thank you."

"I guess I'm not used to being around sick people," I admit.

"Get used to it," my aunt tells me. "This is probably just the tip of the iceberg."

Lydia frowns.

Sid laughs. "Sorry, that's an American saying. It means this is just the beginning of something."

"Oh." Lydia laughs. "I know lots of American sayings, but I don't remember that one, probably because we have no icebergs in New Guinea. You're right; it's a small beginning, but even a small beginning is better than no beginning."

I smile to myself. Okay, maybe she doesn't really get the iceberg meaning, or maybe she's just an optimist, but I have to appreciate her positive attitude.

FOUR

ello, ladies," says a short, white-haired man coming our
way with his hand extended.

"Dr. Larson," says Lydia happily, "here are our new American
friends, Miss Sidney Chase and Miss Maddie Chase."

"Please, use our first names," says my aunt as she shakes the doctor's hand.

"Welcome to Saint Luke's," he says with a British accent. "I
assume you've had the tour."

Sid nods. "Yes, Lydia is a wonderful tour guide."

He smiles at Lydia. "Lydia is a wonderful soul."

"If you'll excuse me now," she says shyly.

"Of course."

We thank her, and she heads back into the clinic. As I watch her
go inside, I am assaulted with guilt. What is wrong with me? Why
can't I be more like her? A Christian should be willing to give and
serve like she's doing. And yet I turned into a basket case just now. I'm
so pathetic.

Dr. Larson points to a table and chairs over in the shade. "Shall
we take a short break over there?"

"Sounds good," says Sid. We go sit with him in the shade, and I must admit that being outside feels a lot better. My breathing seems to be returning to normal. Still, I feel like such a wimp. I try to listen as Sid asks the doctor questions about the clinic. She asks about funding, which seems to come from private donations, partially through the Catholic church that started the clinic, as well as from other donors. More recently, USAID has been helping too.

"But there are many worthy causes to fund," he admits. "We are just one small fish in the sea."

"What about preventive medicines?" she asks.

"Too expensive for our limited budgets."

She nods. "Yes, so I've read. How about AIDS-prevention education?"

"Yes, we are trying to do this. We have classes for young people. We are trying to get into schools, but it's not easy. Lydia teaches some of these classes. Perhaps you would like to sit in on one?"

"Tea?" offers Lydia as she joins us with a tray of tea things and a pitcher of water with lemon slices floating on top. She looks at me. "Are you feeling better?"

"Yes, thanks," I tell her. I am so glad to see that pitcher. "Water sounds good."

"Are you unwell?" asks Dr. Larson.

"No," I say quickly. "I mean, my stomach was a little upset, but I'm not used to being in hospitals."

He nods as he studies me. "Are you taking your antimalarial medications?"

"Yes," I tell him, "I took a Malarone pill at lunchtime, just before we came here."

"That could be part of the reason for nausea," he says.

"That's right," agrees Sid. "It is one of the side effects."

"Really?" I feel hopeful.

"Maybe that's your problem," she says.

"I was just telling the ladies about the AIDS-awareness classes," says Dr. Larson to Lydia. "Do you have one today?"

"Yes," says Lydia. "It's at five."

I glance at my watch. "Just fifteen minutes."

"Would you like to come?" she asks me.

I glance at Sid, and she nods. "That's an excellent idea."

"It's an hour long," Lydia tells my aunt. "We meet in the office where I work, just across the street and down two blocks."

"Great," says Sid. "I'll come over there when Dr. Larson and I are finished here."

So Lydia and I walk over to the government building, and she takes me to a room that has chairs set up in rows and a chalkboard in the front. "This is where we have the classes," she tells me as she puts some printed handouts on the chairs. "Some of the officials weren't too sure about having them here at first. I think they were worried about how it would look, but now they're fully on board."

"That's good."

She nods. "Yes, people are becoming more aware of the problem. At first everyone thought AIDS was someone else's problem. Soon it will be everyone's problem."

I sit down in a chair in the second row and wait as Lydia writes some notes on the chalkboard. I'm guessing she's writing in the pidgin English she told me about, because it makes no sense to me.

It's 5:05, but besides Lydia and me, the room is empty. "Is anyone coming?" I ask.

"I hope so." She smiles at me. "You will soon learn that time is different in our country. Five can mean five fifteen or five thirty to lots of people. I usually begin the class when I think it's time."

By five fifteen there are four girls in the back. I'm guessing they're in their teens, but it's hard to say. They look nervous, and every once in a while they start giggling. Lydia just smiles at them. Then a couple of guys arrive. They sit on the opposite side of the room, away from the giggling girls. It's nearly five thirty when several others come in. Again the guys sit on one side and the girls on the other. I'm not sure why this is, but I plan on asking Lydia afterward.

Now she begins. Of course, she is speaking to the class in pidgin English, but it's interesting to watch her expressions as she gives out information. At times the room is so quiet I can hear people breathing. And then at times the class erupts into laughter. Lydia must be a good teacher.

Just as I assume the class is coming to an end, Lydia becomes very earnest in the way she's talking to them. It appears that she's telling a personal story—perhaps about a patient at the clinic. And then she even cries. I glance around and see some of the others crying too. I so want to know what she's saying to them. But whatever it is, she seems to be getting through to them. Finally she makes some kind of appeal, and she makes it with urgency. She looks around the room as if waiting for a response, and I notice some of them nodding their heads, then looking down at their laps as if they are uncomfortable. After she says a few more things, the class comes to an end.

Lydia talks to some of the girls afterward. They seem very interested in what she says, and I think they are asking her questions. She hands out more printed material and thanks them for coming. Then I notice Dr. Larson and Sid coming in the back door.

"How did it go?" asks Dr. Larson.

Lydia smiles at him. "Good, I think."

I nod in affirmation. "I think it went really well. Lydia seems to be a very good teacher."

"Truly?" says Lydia.

Then I laugh. "Well, I didn't understand a word of it, but it looked like your students appreciated it."

She smiles. "That's good."

"Thank you," Sid says to Lydia and Dr. Larson. "You both have been very helpful."

"I just wish I knew what you told your class," I say to Lydia.

She nods but doesn't offer an explanation.

"Why don't you all join me for dinner?" says Dr. Larson.

"Oh, we don't want to trouble you," my aunt protests, although I can tell she really wants to go.

"It's no trouble." He winks at her. "I have a cook at my house. I will ring her and tell her to expect company." He looks at Lydia now. "You will come too?"

She looks slightly uncomfortable, as if she's embarrassed.

"Please," I say to her, "it will give me a chance to ask you some more questions."

She nods. "Okay. Then I will come."

Dr. Larson gives Sid his home address, which isn't far from the clinic, and tells us to come at seven. "Is that too soon?" he asks, glancing at his watch.

"That's perfect," she says.

We have just enough time to go back to the hotel and freshen up. We arrive at his place just a few minutes after seven. "It's okay," I assure Sid as we get out of the taxi in front of an apartment complex. "Island time is always slow."

She laughs. "I see you're already figuring things out."

As we eat a simple dinner of fish and vegetables, followed by a dessert of fruit and custard, Dr. Larson tells us about himself. He studied tropical medicine in the late fifties and started his practice in New Guinea shortly after that. "I met my wife over here," he says. "She was from America. She came here as a missionary nurse, and I stole her from the Nazarenes." He chuckles. "Of course, I quickly put her to work with me here in Port Moresby. We practiced medicine together for more than thirty years, raised our children here, and finally we retired back to England in 1992."

"But you came back?" I say as his cook removes our plates.

"My wife died five years ago. And I discovered I was old and bored, and I missed New Guinea. I had been reading about the growing AIDS crisis, and I decided to come back and see what I could do to help."

"He's helped a lot," says Lydia. "Dr. Larson was instrumental in acquiring Saint Luke's for an AIDS clinic."

"The old clinic was about to be demolished," he tells us. "I thought that was a colossal waste, and I managed to find a few other people who agreed." He looks up at his cook. "Timi, we'll have our tea on the veranda."

Then we go out to a spacious screened porch with comfortable-looking bamboo furniture and a slow-moving paddle fan overhead. "It's nice out here," I say as I sit on a cushioned chair.

He nods. "My wife taught me the beauty of a veranda." He pulls out a pipe. "Do you mind if I smoke?"

No one protests.

"It's one of my few remaining vices, and I only do it upon occasion," he tells us as he taps his tobacco into place.

Dr. Larson and my aunt begin talking AIDS statistics and projections, and I ask Lydia to tell me a little more about her class today.

"Do you mind if we go inside?" she asks me, discreetly waving her hand against the smoke.

"Not at all."

She excuses us, and we go back into the small living room. "I'm sorry," she says to me. "I do not tolerate tobacco smoke. It upsets my stomach."

"That's okay. Remember how I felt at the clinic today?"

"Yes. You understand." Then she tells me about the village she grew up in and how the men would go into a building to smoke and gossip. "I would merely walk by and smell that smoke, and I would feel sick."

I ask her more about her village, and she tells me some interesting stories.

"Where is it located?" I ask.

"In the highlands. About forty kilometers from Mount Hagen. Do you know where that is?"

"No," I admit. "I should look at a map."

"They have some very good sing-sing festivals up there. Do you know what they are?"

"Yes," I say with enthusiasm. "Sid told me about them. We were hoping we might be able to go to one."

"Your timing is perfect," she says. "The largest sing-sing in the country is next weekend. Maybe you and your aunt would like to go with my friend and me. We'll be heading out on Friday."

"Is it safe to drive the roads?"

She smiles as she considers this. "How would you define *safe*?"

I shrug. "I'm not sure."

"I am a Christian," she says in a firm voice. "I must believe that my God is watching over me. There is no other way to live."

I smile at her. "I'm a Christian too. And I'm trying to believe the same thing. But sometimes I get worried."

She nods. "We all do. But don't worry too much, because I'm not offering you a ride in a car up to the highlands. That's not even possible from here. We would have to fly."

"Oh."

"But let me check on some things first."

Then I ask her about her AIDS class. "I'm so curious about what you told them today. It seemed to get their attention."

"I usually start with basic information," she explains. "That's what I write on the chalkboard. I explain how many people in our country are infected right now and how many more will be infected by next year. I want them to understand that the numbers are increasing. I want them to know that everyone should be concerned. Then I talk about how AIDS is most commonly spread—and I speak openly to them. I tell them about sexual contact and how the virus goes directly from one person to another. I also tell them how to protect themselves by using condoms. But I tell them that the only sure way to prevent AIDS is by abstinence."

I nod. "Do they understand?"

"Yes. But it is not always possible. Some of the women are married to men who are not faithful. And some of them are sex workers and don't use any precautions. And some of them have no choice; some of them have been raped, at times by more than one person."

"I've heard about this."

She sighs. "It's very sad."

"How have you learned so much about this?" I ask.

She just shrugs, then changes the subject, telling me about where she grew up in the highlands. She smiles as if she's imagining it. "It's a beautiful place with lush green trees and a rushing river. My village is called Lomokako."

"And how do you speak such good English?" I ask.

"A family from America came to my village long ago."

"Americans live in your village?"

She nods. "The Johnson family came to Lomokako when I was a baby. I believe God sent them to save me."

"They were missionaries?"

"Yes, language workers with SIL."

"SIL?"

"Summer Institute of Linguistics."

"Oh." I'm not sure what this means, but it sounds official.

"They came to learn our tribal language and to translate the Bible for us."

"Really?"

"Yes."

"And that's how you got saved?"

She gets a twinkle in her eye now. "The Johnsons saved me when I was a baby."

"Huh?" I wonder if we're talking about the same thing.

"You see, my father was from Lomokako, but my mother was from another village, and she died when I was born. So my father's sister cared for me. But my father was killed working in the copper mine, and my aunt no longer wanted to care for me because there was no money."

I try to take this in. "That must've been hard for you."

"It is simply what *is*," she says, "in my country."

"So what happened then?" I ask.

"The Johnsons took me into their own home."

"They adopted you?"

"Yes. And they raised me as their own daughter. I have two older brothers: Jeremy and Caleb."

"But your last name isn't Johnson?"

"They named me Lydia, but I kept my father's family name, Obuti. It was my choice, my way to remain connected to my country."

"Wow."

She smiles. "Yes, *wow*. My parents are very good people. They sent my brothers and me away to college in the United States. But they could afford only two years for each of us. After that, we must get scholarships or earn our own tuition. I want to go to medical school, but it's so expensive. I have some scholarship money left, but I must earn more before I go back."

"I'm in my second year of college," I tell her.

"How old are you?"

"I just turned twenty."

"I am twenty-one, soon to be twenty-two."

"I thought you were older," I admit. "You seem very mature."

She frowns slightly. "Some of my friends are already in their fourth year of college."

"But you are going back?"

She looks down at her lap now. "I hope so."

I suspect something is troubling her, but I hate to be a pest. "Well, I could tell the people in your class really respected you today," I say, hoping to cheer her up. "You must be a good teacher."

"I hope so."

"There you ladies are," says Dr. Larson as he and Sid come inside to join us.

"Some of the mosquitoes were sneaking in through the screen," says Sid, pointing to a large red welt on her arm.

"Good that you're taking the antimalarial," says Dr. Larson.

Then Sid looks at her watch. "Thank you for your hospitality," she tells him, "but I think we should let you get some rest."

He nods. "Yes, it seems the older I get, the earlier the morning comes."

Then Sid calls for a taxi, and we offer Lydia a ride.

"Yes," says Dr. Larson in a serious tone, more to Lydia than to us. "Women should *not* go out alone at night." He firmly shakes his head. "It's not safe. Not at all."

FIVE

*T*he next morning the phone in our hotel room rings and wakes me up out of a sound sleep. Sid must be in the bathroom, so I pick it up and mutter, "Hello."

"Hello. Is this Maddie?"

"Yes," I answer groggily.

"This is Lydia Obuti. I'm sorry to bother you, but I got an idea last night."

I sit up and try to focus. "Yes?"

"It might not be a good idea, but I thought I should tell you."

"Go ahead."

"As you know, we're short-handed at the clinic. I thought perhaps you would learn more about AIDS and the problem in our country if you spent some time helping there. Or perhaps you'd just like to talk to the patients. They get so few visitors. It's very lonely for them."

"But I don't speak pidgin," I point out.

"A friend from my village is in town this week. He's the language helper to my parents. I called and told him about you and your aunt. I asked if he could help to translate pidgin for you at the clinic, and he agreed. His English isn't as good as mine, but he's understandable."

"And he doesn't mind helping?"

She sort of laughs. "Let's just say he's willing. And since he's a friend of the family's, maybe he's afraid to say no."

Okay, I'm not sure what this means, but I tell her I think it sounds like a good way for me to do some research. "Let me ask my aunt first," I say as Sid emerges from the bathroom with a towel wrapped around her head.

"Ask me what?" she says.

I explain Lydia's idea, and Sid thinks it sounds good. "I've got some writing to do this morning anyway," she says. "Go ahead." And so I agree to meet Lydia's friend Peter Sampala at Saint Luke's at ten.

"This is really a great opportunity," says Sid as she towels her hair. "You can get some first-person accounts that I can excerpt. That Lydia is really a smart girl."

I fill Sid in a bit on Lydia's history, how she was adopted by the Johnsons. "She wants to go to med school," I say, "but she has to earn tuition first."

"Wow, that's got to be a challenge." Then Sid gets that light-bulb look on her face. "But what if someone partnered with her to support her financially? For instance, my editor, who has no children of his own but has a big heart for Papua New Guinea? What a great way to invest in this country's future."

"That's a very cool idea."

"Or maybe my church?" she says. "They're always looking for some new kind of international outreach." I can see the wheels spinning in her brain as she skims over the room-service menu.

"Maybe my church too," I suggest. "Maybe our youth group could do some fund-raisers."

"Let's have breakfast in the room today." Sid tosses the menu to me. "I don't feel like getting dressed this morning."

I order our breakfast and take a shower, and then we discuss Lydia's future a bit more while we eat. Strange as it sounds, it seems that Lydia's chance of being adopted more than once in her lifetime is becoming a distinct possibility.

"But let's not tell her for a while," says Sid as she sips her coffee. "Just see how it goes. Besides, I'd like to check some things out back home first."

"Sure," I agree. "No sense in getting her hopes up."

"Well, you should probably head over to the clinic now, Maddie." She studies me with a concerned look. "Are you sure you want to do this?"

"Why not?"

"Well, remember how you got kind of sick to your stomach when we were there yesterday?"

"That might've been from the Malarone," I point out.

"Speaking of which…" She gets up and goes to her purse for our pills.

"Besides, I was thinking about it," I say as she gives me a pill. "You know, I grew up on a farm. I've shoveled everything imaginable. I've helped deliver calves and lambs and foals. I've buried dead animals. I don't think being in that clinic should get to me like it seemed to yesterday."

She nods now. "You're probably right. To be honest, I was feeling a little queasy in Sydney, and that was the second day we took the malaria pills."

"So," I proclaim, "that's what I'm going to blame it on."

"Good for you."

"It was really bugging me to think that I couldn't handle being around sick people like that," I admit. "I mean it seems so shallow and selfish. Yesterday I kept thinking, what would Jesus do?"

She smiles sadly. "Heal them?"

"Don't you wish?"

"Well, good luck. And don't forget to take lots of notes."

I pick up my notebook, then slip it into my bag.

"Let me get you some kinas for the taxi or whatnot," she says, getting into her purse. "And do not walk anywhere by yourself, Maddie. Do you understand?"

I nod. "Yes."

"Take my cell phone too." She hands me her phone and the money. "Don't be afraid to use my phone if you need to. In fact, why don't you give me a call to let me know when you get there and when you're coming back. Do you have the hotel phone number?"

I pick up a piece of notepaper from the desk. "It's on this."

"Okay." She looks carefully at me. "Get a bottle of water from the lobby too. Just to have in your bag."

"Anything else?" I say with impatience. "Should I take a sleeping bag or a survival kit or maybe a handgun?"

"Sorry. But we have to be careful. You are taking me seriously, aren't you?"

I salute her. "Yes ma'am. Of course, ma'am."

She rolls her eyes. "And only ride in a taxi that you have called for,

Maddie. Make sure they know who you are before you get in, and make sure it is a properly marked taxi."

"I know this already," I remind her.

"Yeah, yeah." She waves me away now. "Go on. But do be careful!"

"I promise, I will be extremely careful."

Then, feeling as if I'm going off to battle, I ride down the elevator and walk into the lobby. Honestly, I find that I'm looking over my shoulder as I go. It's like paranoia is kicking in, and I'm thinking I'm about to be abducted. I tell myself to just chill, but I do follow my aunt's explicit directions. First I go to the concierge and ask him to call me a taxi. Then I go and buy a bottle of water. And a chocolate bar, just in case. Then I go and wait until the taxi pulls up. I don't get in until the driver politely asks if I am Missis Chase. Okay, maybe I'm not a *missis,* but I've noticed the nationals seem to call all women that. So I say a silent prayer and get in.

At first I feel a slight wave of apprehension when the driver takes a different route than we took yesterday. I'm actually about to say something, but then he turns down a street I recognize, and before I know it, I'm in front of the clinic. Seems he knew a shortcut. So I pay him and thank him and get out. He smiles brightly at me, and not for the first time, I think what a naturally friendly people New Guineans are—and why do we have to be so careful?

But as I'm walking up to the front door of the clinic, I see another New Guinean man. This guy is loitering on the sidewalk and glancing around in a nervous sort of way. He's got a short beard and is wearing a brightly colored shirt, but he seems to be watching me with a little too much interest. Suddenly I feel pretty uptight. So instead of looking directly at him, I hurry past and go straight into the clinic, practically running it seems. Once I'm inside, I can feel my heart pounding, and although it's probably just my imagination, I feel that I've just escaped some sort of great peril.

"Missis Chase?" says a male voice behind me. I turn around, expecting to see the friendly taxi driver. Perhaps I left something in his car. But instead it's the man in the bright shirt—the one I've just escaped from. I frown at him.

"I'm sorry. Are you Missis Chase?"

"Yes," I say cautiously.

"I am Peter Sampala. I am a friend of Lydia Obuti. She told me to meet you here."

"Oh," I say in relief. "I'm sorry. I didn't mean to run from you like that."

"No," he says in a serious tone. "That is good. You should not talk to strangers."

I smile. "Yes, I know that."

He looks somewhat relieved but still a bit uneasy. I'm afraid I offended him when I all but ran away from him screaming for help. Still, he seems to understand.

"Have you been here before?" I ask.

He shakes his head. "No. Lydia works here sometimes, and I have picked her up after, but I have not been inside."

"Hallo," says one of the nurses that I met yesterday. "Can I help you?"

"This is Peter Sampala," I say, glad that I can remember his last name and hoping I pronounced it correctly. "Lydia Obuti asked me to come—"

"I know. I know," she interrupts. "You are to talk to patients." She nods in the direction where someone is yelling. It sounds like the person is calling for help. "I am very busy. You will have to find your own way today."

"Oh, that's okay," I start to say, but she is already heading down the hall. I glance back to Peter, who is looking even more uneasy now. "Are you ready?"

He nods, but I can tell by the way he's looking around—his eyes darting down one hallway and then the other—that he doesn't want to be here.

"Do you mind doing this?" I say as I begin to walk down the hall toward the patients' rooms.

He takes a quick breath and looks like he's about to make a run for it. Perhaps he's as frightened of me as I was of him. Or maybe it's something else. I pause by one of the rooms, about to go in, but he hesitates in the hallway. "Do you want to come in?"

He nods again, taking a careful step, then hesitating.

"Does it bother you to be here?" I ask him in a quiet tone.

"Yes. A little."

"I have an idea," I say. "Let's go out to the courtyard and have a quick talk." Then I lead him to the exit we used yesterday, going to the same bench where I thought I was going to lose my lunch. "Sit down," I tell him.

He does, and I sit down beside him. "Look," I begin, "I was here yesterday, and it made me uncomfortable too."

He nods as if taking this in.

"And I'm not used to being around sick people either. I think I was a little scared."

"Sick people are not so bad," he begins in a quiet tone. "But AIDS…it is bad. Very bad."

"Oh."

"People with AIDS…they are not Christian people. Good people do not get this terrible disease. This is God's judgment on these people because they chose sin and not God. It is bad…bad…"

I consider this. For some reason his thinking rings a bell with me. And then it hits me. I remember something I read in Margaret Mead's book. Sure it happened long ago, but perhaps it's still part of the culture here today. People used to believe that if someone did something wrong and refused to confess it, that person or someone close to him would get sick and maybe even die. They thought there was a direct correlation between sin and sickness. Time and again, Margaret Mead actually observed this very thing happening in the village she was visiting. Maybe that's what Peter was concerned about here.

"Do you think that everyone who has AIDS has done something wrong?" I ask, just wanting to be sure that I'm clear.

He nods eagerly. "Yes."

"And you think they have AIDS because they are bad people?"

Again he nods. "Yes. We all know this to be true."

"Have you ever discussed this with Lydia?"

"No." He frowns down at his feet.

I wish Lydia were here. I'm sure she could explain this better than I can. "But do you know that little children get AIDS?"

He just keeps looking at his feet.

"You think it's because they sin?"

"It's because of sin."

"Oh."

He looks at me now. "It is evil, this AIDS. God does not want his people to get this evil sickness. He does not want his people to be near this sin. I should not be here now."

"Do you believe in Jesus?" I ask.

"Yes!" He nods his head firmly. "I do believe in Jesus."

"What do you think Jesus would do if he were here? What would he do if he saw these sick people?"

Peter looks down at his feet again.

"I can't make you come inside and talk with the patients," I tell him. "But maybe you should ask Jesus what he would want you to do."

He lets out a long sigh but keeps looking down.

"I don't speak pidgin English," I tell him. "So without your help, I won't be able to hear their stories."

He's still looking at his feet. And suddenly I remember that I forgot to call Sid and tell her I'm here. I'm surprised she hasn't called me, but when I look, I see that the phone is turned off.

"Excuse me," I tell him. "I need to make a phone call."

I call Sid and explain the situation.

"Maybe you should just come back," she says, still sounding worried.

I glance over to where Peter is still sitting on the bench, his head hanging down. "Not yet," I tell her. "Maybe Peter will come around."

"Keep me posted."

I hang up and wait a couple of minutes as I silently pray for God to open Peter's eyes right now. I pray that God will help this confused man to see that many of the people who are sick with AIDS have simply been victims. And perhaps God could show Peter that forgiveness is available to everyone, including those who got AIDS through bad choices. As I pray, I begin to understand what could possibly be one of the problems with this AIDS epidemic: it might be that well-meaning but fearful people like Peter don't understand what's really going on.

SIX

I go back to Peter and ask him whether he wants to translate for me this morning.

"I believe Jesus would help these people," Peter says in a sad voice.

I smile. "That's good."

"But I am still worried."

"Why?"

He looks up at me with frightened eyes. "I do not want the AIDS sickness. I have a wife and baby back in my village. I do not want to take this sickness to them."

I nod. This concern is much easier to handle. "You can't catch AIDS from these people, Peter. You won't get it by talking to them. Not even if you touch them."

"Do you know this for sure?"

"Yes," I tell him, "I've learned about it in my country." He still looks uncertain. "Hasn't Lydia told you this?"

He shrugs now. "Maybe."

"So, do you want to do this with me, Peter? Are you all right?"

"I will try. I will pray for Jesus to be in me."

I smile at him. "Yes, that's what I'll do too."

Then he stands up. "I know that Jesus healed people. He touched people with leprosy. That is a bad illness too."

"Is there leprosy in New Guinea?" I ask as we walk toward the entrance.

"A little. Not so much as the AIDS."

The first room we go into has three women in it. I think this might be better than a ward, which is overwhelming to me and might really frighten Peter. I go to the woman whose bed is near the window. She is looking outside with a very sad expression. I can see that she is a pretty woman, maybe about my age or even younger, but her face and arms have lots of open sores, which are even more visible due to her skin tone, which is about the color of cocoa.

For a split second I can relate to Peter. I so don't want to touch this woman. To be honest, I don't even want to be here right now. To make matters worse, I'm starting to feel a wave of nausea coming on. This is not good. So I tell myself just to chill, remembering how it's probably the Malarone pill I took with breakfast. Still, it does make me wonder how bad malaria can be if taking these pills makes me feel this lousy. I look at the woman and realize that she probably feels way worse than I do.

I take a steadying breath and scoot a chair next to this woman's bed and ask if I can sit down. Peter translates this into pidgin, and the woman looks slightly surprised, but she nods her head with a tired sigh. Then I introduce myself to her and tell her I'm from the United States, and she tells us that her name is Mary Kilamo and that she is from a village near the town of Goroka.

"I'm working on a news article about the AIDS epidemic in

Papua New Guinea," I begin slowly, waiting for Peter to translate this as I take out my notebook and write down her name.

She gives me a blank look, almost as if she is bored or maybe just tired, and I ask Peter if she understands what he just told her.

He nods.

"And I want to get stories of real people," I continue, "people like you who have AIDS. Do you mind if I ask you some questions?"

Peter translates this, and the woman from the bed on the other side of Mary makes a comment, which I can't understand. I glance at Peter, who looks slightly exasperated. "It was nothing," he says. "Nothing you want to hear."

"Did she say something bad?" I ask.

"I think she's jealous," he tells me. "She wants you to talk to her instead of Mary."

I turn and force a stiff smile at the plump woman, who doesn't look nearly as sick as Mary. In fact, she looks perfectly fine, and I wonder why she's here taking up valuable space. "Tell her I will talk to her *after* Mary," I say, and Peter quickly dispenses this message to her. She nods and smiles smugly at me.

Then I look back at Mary. "How are you feeling today?"

"No *goot*," she says without waiting for Peter to translate.

"Do you speak English?" I ask.

"*Nogat*."

"Oh." I smile at her. "But maybe you understand it a little?"

The corners of her mouth almost turn up into a smile but not quite. Then she slowly nods.

"How long have you been in the clinic?" I ask, and Peter translates.

"Three months," he tells me, and I write it down.

Then I ask if her family comes to visit her, and I discover they do not. So I ask about friends and learn that she has none. I ask how old she is and find out she's twenty-three. Then I ask how long she's had AIDS, and she tells us she got it when she was eleven. I feel shocked at this. She's not much older than I am, but she has had AIDS for twelve years, more than half of her life. I tell her that I'm sorry and that it's too bad. As I say this, I can feel tears in my eyes, and I don't even try to hide them.

"Do you mind if I ask how you got AIDS?"

Peter translates and then waits for what is a fairly long answer. But after she's done speaking, he just sits there for an even longer time. His face is expressionless, and I assume he's trying to reword her response into English for me. But when he begins to tell me her answer, I see that he, too, has tears in his eyes. I can tell this is difficult for him.

"She says it happened in her village when she was a young girl. She and her friend were supposed to be working in the garden, which is away from the village, but they were playing like children do. And they were careless, too near a public road. A band of men found them and took the girls away in a truck. They took them far from home. And then the men raped both the girls. Many times." He takes in a sharp breath and continues. "Her friend was killed. But Mary did not die. After some time—she does not remember how long—she became sick, and the men let her go."

Tears are running freely down my cheeks now, and despite my earlier revulsion, I take Mary's hand in mine and tell her that I'm so sorry. She seems to understand this without translation. Peter also says he is sorry, but he remains where he's sitting. He doesn't touch her. That's okay, maybe even for the best. I make some quick notes, planning to fill in more details later.

Then she says something else, and Peter translates for me. "That was a long time ago." It's as if she's trying to make us feel better.

I nod. "Yes. But what happened after that? After the men let you go, did you return to your home?"

Peter translates, and I learn that, yes, she did return to her home. But she returned in shame. Her family was disgusted with her. They told her to leave, that she was not welcome. She was worthless to them. Dead.

I remember something I recently read about New Guinean culture. Daughters have monetary value because their families can get a bride price when they are married. In other words, the groom must pay the bride's father with livestock and produce and other goods in order to marry her. Depending on the girl, the price can go quite high. Seeing that Mary is a very pretty girl, I'm guessing her family had great hopes for her. I'm guessing she was an investment that lost its value.

"Was she considered worthless because a daughter's value is related to the bride price?" I ask Peter in a quiet voice.

Peter sadly nods, thankfully without even translating my words to Mary. I can tell he's familiar with this custom. Perhaps he even had to come up with a bride price for his own wife. But poor Mary. Just because she was raped and hurt, she lost everything. It's so sad. So unfair.

"What did you do after your family sent you away?" I ask. I realize I'm still holding her hand, but she doesn't seem to mind.

She tells us that she stayed with relatives in another village. They made her work for food. But it wasn't long before they, too, did not want her around. And so she came to the city, to Port Moresby.

"And what did you do here?" I ask.

Peter translates, and she pulls her hand away from mine and looks down at her lap. I can tell she's ashamed.

The woman from the next bed laughs and says something to Peter, something that seems to embarrass him. He looks away. Mary looks uncomfortable too. She turns and looks out the window again.

"What did that woman say?" I ask Peter.

He leans over and speaks quietly to me. "She said Mary was a sex worker." He turns and scowls at the woman. "She used different words, cruel words, but that is what she said."

"It's not surprising," I tell him. "She had no family, no friends, no education, and her future was ruined."

He frowns and looks at the floor. I can tell this isn't easy for him, and I thank him for his patience and his help.

"It's all right," he says.

"I want to tell her about a woman in the Bible—the one caught in sin, the one Jesus defended."

His eyes brighten now. "I know that story, Missis Chase. I translate that story for Mister and Missis Johnson. I can tell her that story."

And so I sit and listen as Peter tells the story. I don't understand the words, but I can almost tell what he's saying by his hand movements and expressions.

"I told her how no one threw a stone," he says.

"That's great!" I tell him. "Did you say that Jesus forgave her?"

So he goes on to tell her more. I watch Mary as she listens, and somehow I think she understands the significance. And then he stops and looks at me.

"Did you tell her that Jesus wants to forgive her too?"

"I almost forgot." And then he begins to talk with excitement, telling her that last bit. His eyes light up as he continues. I'm not sure what he's saying, but Mary is listening intently. In fact, it seems the other women are listening rather intently too.

Then Peter turns and looks at me with an almost-radiant expression. "She wants to pray with us. She wants to invite Jesus into her heart. She wants to receive his forgiveness."

I'm nodding now, and I take Mary's hand. "Yes," I say to Peter, "let's pray with her. Can you do this?"

"Yes. I am also a pastor for our village church. I know how to pray this prayer. We pray it often in our church."

And so we bow our heads, and Peter prays, and Mary echoes his words, and finally he says "amen." And when I look up, Mary is quietly crying. But she is also smiling.

"Tell Mary that she is our sister in Christ now," I say with excitement. This is so amazing. I mean I've been a Christian for years, but I've never experienced anything quite like this before.

Mary nods after Peter tells her she's our sister. Then she leans back against her pillow and takes in a deep breath. She closes her eyes, and I sense that she's tired. I hope we haven't worn her out. We all sit there quietly for a couple of minutes.

"Maybe we should go," I say to Peter. "Ask her if she needs to get some rest. But tell her we'd like to come back and talk to her some more."

So he does this, and she nods and says something.

"She wants us to come back later," he says. "She is tired."

Then the woman in the next bed speaks again. And Peter tells me that she is ready to talk now.

"Tell her we'll come back later for her story," I say, thinking I'd rather not talk to her at all if possible. "Tell her I need to write some things down first so I don't forget."

He nods and speaks to the woman, who clearly looks disappointed, but I don't really care. I tell Mary good-bye, and we leave. I head straight back outside to the courtyard, feeling the need for some fresh air and sunshine. We go over to the table and chairs and sit down.

"You did a good thing in there," I tell Peter as I open my notebook.

He nods and smiles. "I know. God was with us, Missis Chase."

"Are you glad you changed your mind about talking to someone with AIDS?" I ask, even though it seems obvious.

"Thank you for helping me, Missis Chase."

"Thank *you!*"

Peter sits there humming as I write some more notes, and when I'm done, I realize it's close to noon. "I need to call my aunt," I tell him. So I call Sid and tell her what's happening here.

"Do you want to stay longer?" she asks.

"Just a minute," I say. Then I ask Peter if he has more time to translate for me, and he eagerly agrees. "Yes," I tell her. "It's going so well, maybe we should just keep at it."

"I have an idea," she tells me. "I'll bring you guys some lunch. How does that sound?"

"Great!"

Then Peter and I go back and interview a young man named Manoa, whose story is just as sad as Mary's. And in some ways it is much worse. He, too, was kidnapped as a child. He was sexually abused and beaten. When police found him, instead of returning him to his family, they locked him up. And there his abuse continued. Unfortunately, Manoa is very bitter about all this. And, really, who can blame him? Even when Peter tries to tell him about Jesus, Manoa doesn't want to hear it. He holds up his hands and tells Peter about how he went to the church for help once, but the Christians turned him away.

"Tell him that not all Christians are like that," I instruct Peter. "Tell him there are Christians who would accept him and love him the way Jesus does."

Peter nods sadly, and I can tell that he's feeling bad about some of his own previous prejudices. Perhaps he has been one of those Christians himself, the kind who would turn someone like Manoa or Mary away. But he's changing. It's obvious to see he's changing.

Sid comes with our lunches, and we go outside to eat and visit with her. Peter, with great enthusiasm, tells her all about Mary and how she accepted Jesus into her heart.

"I wonder if Christians ever come to see the patients here?" says Sid as we're finishing our lunches.

"I can ask Lydia," I offer. "I'm sure she would know."

"Lydia visits with the patients," says Peter, almost as if the meaning of this is just hitting him. "She is a good Christian."

"Maybe people need to get the word out," I tell Peter. "Christians need to hear about what you experienced today."

He nods solemnly. "Yes. I will go out and tell them my story. I will tell them how I have changed. I will challenge them to change with me. I will remind them of Jesus and the ten lepers."

SEVEN

fter lunch, my aunt goes over some things with Dr. Larson while Peter and I return to Mary's room. She's had a nap and food and seems to be feeling stronger now. We visit with her some more, and Peter promises to send other Christians to talk to her. He even asks if she would like a Bible, but she says she can't read very well.

The woman in the bed next to Mary demands our attention. She insists on being heard. So I move my chair over by her bed, and, trying to hide my exasperation, I begin to ask her the same sorts of questions, and Peter patiently translates for me. Her name is Pilada, and I soon discover that her story is a bit different from the others. She got AIDS from her husband, although she's not sure how long it has been, because he still hasn't shown symptoms. She was discovered to be positive only about a year ago. Based on her history, her husband was tested shortly after that. Naturally, she is certain her husband got HIV/AIDS from someone just like Mary. And it's not out of the question. It also explains her animosity toward her roommate.

But as I take notes and listen to Pilada share her story, I get the feeling that her attitude toward Mary is changing. At one point, when Mary begins to cough uncontrollably, Pilada stops talking and insists that I go and assist the girl. I help Mary drink some water and give her some tissues, and after she quiets down, I return to Pilada, who seems satisfied that I tended to Mary. But it convinces me that Pilada feels compassion now. Maybe it's from overhearing Mary's story about being raped as a girl. Or maybe it's simply the fact that Peter and I both showed Mary some respect.

We learn that Pilada's AIDS hasn't progressed as far as Mary's, but it's been complicated by another illness she's had since her first pregnancy. About twelve years ago, she began to suffer from diabetes. She's received some treatment for it because her husband is employed by a corporation that, amazingly, has limited health benefits. But if her health doesn't stabilize soon, the combo of AIDS and diabetes leaves her with a pretty poor prognosis.

"She has five children between the ages of four and twelve," Peter translates in a serious voice.

I look at this woman—the same woman I had been irritated with because of her bossiness—and I realize she has a lot at stake. No wonder she feels out of sorts. "Tell her I hope that her health stabilizes soon."

He says this, and she thanks me.

"How are her children doing?" I ask Peter. "Find out if any of them have HIV or if they've been tested."

He asks her and then frowns as she gives her answer. He turns back to me. "They've all been tested," he says. "Two of them, the younger ones, have HIV. But they don't have symptoms yet."

"I'm sorry," I tell Pilada. The word *sorry* is the same in pidgin, so she understands my meaning. "That is very sad." I turn to Peter. "Ask her who cares for her children while she's getting treatment." So he does, and she talks for a while, then he tells me that her mother and sister and sister-in-law all help out. Their village is about a hundred kilometers from here, so she doesn't get to see her children. And no one from the village knows she has the virus. They think she's here only because her diabetes has gotten worse.

"Ask how her family and friends would react if they knew she and her family had AIDS."

He translates this, and her dark brown eyes grow large with fear and realization. She does not answer him, but her hand flies over her mouth, and for the first time today, she is totally speechless.

"Tell her that we won't tell anyone," I say quickly. "Assure her that anything she says here will be our secret. Make her understand."

So Peter begins talking quickly, explaining our plan for anonymity, and soon I see relief washing over her face.

"*Tenkyu, tenkyu,*" she says to me again and again.

Finally we wrap up this interview, and I thank Pilada for telling us her story, once again reassuring her that we will change her name when the story is retold. "People need to hear these true stories," I explain to both her and Mary. "It helps them to understand that real people are hurt by this disease." Then, to my amazement, Peter asks Pilada if she is a Christian. She confirms that she is, and then he asks her if she has a Bible, which she says she does not, although she proudly tells us that she *can* read.

"I will see that you get a Bible," Peter says, "if you will promise to read it to Mary too."

She considers this and finally nods in agreement. I think Peter should consider becoming a diplomat.

The third woman in their room is asleep now. She has been sleeping for most of the day. The few times she was awake, she was quiet. Judging by her emaciated appearance, her open sores, and sunken eyes, I suspect her condition is the most advanced.

We get a few more interviews, and finally I think it's time to stop. I thank Peter for his translation help. "You have been really amazing," I tell him, and he smiles shyly.

"Thank you for helping me," he says.

"Hello," calls a woman's voice. We turn to see Lydia walking toward us. She looks neat and clean in her navy-blue skirt and a light blue blouse. I'm guessing she's just gotten off work. "How is it going?" she asks as she joins us. "Have you met very many patients?"

I go over the list of the ones we interviewed, and she seems impressed. "That's excellent." She turns to Peter now. "How did you like doing this?"

He quickly and honestly explains his earlier concerns and fears, and she nods and seems to understand. "I'm so glad you stayed and helped."

"I am glad too."

"And I'm glad I caught you before you left," she says. "I told Maddie about the Mount Hagen Sing-Sing."

His eyes light up. "Do you and your aunt want to see it?"

"We would love to see it."

"I will fly to the highlands tomorrow," he says. "The JAARS flight is not full. So you and your aunt can come, if you want."

"I'm going too," says Lydia.

"Yes, of course." He nods, then turns to me. "Lydia is like my own niece. Her parents have been so good to me and my family."

She smiles. "Yes, we are all like family. And you should see his little girl, Hannah. She is adorable."

He frowns. "Do not remind me. I am missing her too much already."

"One more day," says Lydia, "and you will see her."

Just then I notice my aunt and Dr. Larson coming our way. I wave to Sid, and when she joins us, I tell her about this great opportunity to go to the Mount Hagen Sing-Sing with Peter and Lydia.

"You can't miss that," says Dr. Larson. "It's the biggest festival of the year. You're very fortunate to be here during August."

"We'd love to go," says Sid. "But do you think we'll be able to get hotel accommodations at this late date?"

"No," says Lydia with a twinkle in her eye. "The hotels will probably be fully booked. But I think I can find you a place to stay."

"Really?" Sid looks a little unsure, as if she's imagining herself sleeping on the dirt floor of a hut.

"My parents have room in their house. My brothers are both in the States right now. You can come and stay with us."

"Thank you," says Sid. "That's so generous."

"You won't be sorry," says Dr. Larson. "I've gone dozens of times, and it's one of the few events that preserves some of the true flavors of this country." He chuckles. "Make sure you take a camera and lots of film."

"Would you like to join us, Dr. Larson?" offers Lydia.

"No, no." He shakes his head. "I fear I'm getting too old for such adventures."

We try to argue this point, and then, laughing, he excuses himself for an appointment.

"What time is the flight, Peter?" asks Lydia.

"Not until one. I have to take care of some tasks in the morning," he says. He glances at us. "I am here to do work for Lydia's parents."

"How's the printing coming along?" asks Lydia.

"Good," he says.

"It's my parents' New Testament for our village," Lydia explains. "They finished their translation in March and then spent the next two months checking it. It's being printed here in Port Moresby this very week. That's why Peter is here. He's making sure it all comes together just right."

"How exciting," says Sid.

"Yes," agrees Lydia. "They're planning a dedication celebration for the weekend after this. That is, if the New Testaments are on schedule."

"Everything looks good for that," says Peter.

So we agree that Peter will pick up Sid and me at the hotel tomorrow, and then we'll swing by Lydia's apartment.

"I have a borrowed car here," Peter says to Sid and me. "Do you want a ride back to your hotel now?"

"That would be great," says Sid.

"I better go do my visiting before some of the patients get impatient." Lydia smiles and waves good-bye. Then we follow Peter out to his car, which he tells us belongs to some friends of Lydia's parents. "They are very generous with the car," he explains as we get into the old Toyota. "Many translators use it while they are in Port Moresby."

"It's a lot better than riding in a taxi," says Sid as she gets into the front seat.

"Yes." He nods. "I was concerned for your niece this morning, Missis Chase. The taxi driver was too friendly with her."

"Really?" I ask from the backseat. "How do you know that?"

"I can tell by his face." Peter's voice grows more serious. "Women from other countries do not always know what is right for our people. What you might think is friendliness, a young man might think is…something else."

"See," says Sid, "that's just what I was trying to get across to you, Maddie. You're a pretty young woman, and if you smile at some young man, he might interpret that as a come-on."

Okay, now I'm feeling embarrassed. No way was I trying to come on to the taxi driver. Or anyone else.

"Best to be careful," warns Peter. "Watch out for strangers."

"Thank you," says Sid. "That's exactly what I've been trying to make Maddie understand."

Well, fine. I lean back into the seat, feeling like a five-year-old who's just been reprimanded.

"My people do not understand Americans," Peter continues. I lean forward now, interested in what he's telling us. "American movies and television tell my people that Americans have no morals, that they do not have Christian values."

"But that's not true," I point out.

"I know this," he says. "I know this because I have the Johnsons. They show me by the way they live that Americans are not wicked."

"But New Guineans think Americans are wicked?" asks Sid.

"Yes, I am sorry to say this is true." He shakes his head as he pulls up to our hotel. "The trouble is that many people in my country want to act like these wicked Americans more than they want to act like Jesus. It is not good."

"No," says Sid, "it is not good."

We thank Peter for the ride and tell him that we'll see him tomorrow, then go into the hotel.

"It's sad, isn't it?" I say as we wait for the elevator.

She nods. "Yes. In some ways I suppose that Americans and Western culture in general could be blamed for a lot of the problems in this country."

"Like the AIDS epidemic?"

"Yes." The elevator bell rings, the door opens, and two Caucasian businessmen walk out.

I remember how Margaret Mead compared the New Guineans to children, but I don't say this as we ride up. Even so I'm curious. It seems quite likely that white people came in here and sort of took over, perhaps even took unfair advantage.

"It's the same old story." Sid sighs. "Colonialism in third-world countries initially brings benefits like medicine, education, economic development, Christianity…but for every good thing, a lot of bad stuff seems to be dragged along as well. Things like exposure to immorality, alcohol and drugs, crime, greed…"

"Does it ever make you wonder whether it's worth it or not?" I say as we get out of the elevator.

"That's the great global question," she says as she unlocks the door to our room. "You answer that one, and you might be able to rule the world, Maddie."

"Or get permanently kicked out."

We both laugh as we go into our room.

"Let's have a little rest," says Sid as she kicks off her shoes and turns on the big overhead paddle fan, our form of air conditioning. "Kind of regroup and go over our notes. And then we have a guy from USAID who wants to take us to dinner and give us a little tour this evening."

So I go over my notes from interviews, filling in some things I didn't have time to write down. Then I use Sid's computer to enter my stories. I feel really good about the information I gathered today. I think she should find some material that will be useful to her article.

Before I turn off the computer, I go online to check my e-mail. Still nothing from Ryan. Now I'm starting to get really worried. I wonder if I said something to offend him before I left. He'd pretended to be jealous of me for getting to take this trip with Sid, and, naturally, I played it up some. But it all seemed to be just good fun. Now I'm not so sure. I hope everything is okay with him.

EIGHT

M r. Osterman meets us in the hotel lobby at five thirty. He's an older man, not as old as Dr. Larson, but I'm guessing he might be close to sixty. Even so, I can't help but notice that he's being extra nice to my aunt as he helps her into the car. I also notice that he's not wearing a wedding band. Of course, this reminds me of good old Ian, back in Ireland, and I want to tell Mr. Osterman to take a number and get in line. Naturally, I don't do this. Although I do remember my aunt's little speech to me this afternoon about leading guys on. Yeah, right. Okay, I realize this is different. Mr. Osterman isn't a New Guinean, and my aunt's not leading him on, but I can still give her a hard time later just for fun.

Sid fills him in on what we've seen and done so far, which really isn't much, but then, we've been here less than two days.

"Maddie did some wonderful research over at Saint Luke's today," she's saying now, and my ears perk up.

"What sort of research?" he asks as he takes a road that seems to lead away from the city.

"She's been interviewing patients with AIDS. I just started reading over some of your notes, Maddie," she calls back to me, "while

83

you were in the shower. And they were very impressive. You've made some really good observations, and I can't wait to incorporate them into my article."

"Thanks." I can't help but feel pleased. Who knew?

Sid turns back to Mr. Osterman now. "It's like Maddie is putting a human face on this disease. Making it real and personal."

"That's super," he says. "So much of what we read about the AIDS crisis is simply statistics and dismal forecasts. We hardly ever get to hear the personal side of the tragedy."

"Exactly," says Sid. "And I think a lot of Americans can't relate to third-world countries in the first place. It's almost like they're hearing about aliens from another planet."

"Planet Poverty," he says.

"That's it," says Sid. "Americans don't understand poverty like this."

"And yet we're the most generous country in the world," says Mr. Osterman. "So many programs are funded by U.S. dollars—whether it's charitable donations or government grants."

"I think a lot of it is *guilt* giving," says Sid.

He nods. "Yes, it seems that people open their purses faster than they open their hearts."

"Well, perhaps we can help open their eyes."

"Good for you."

Then we drive along quietly for a couple of minutes, and I realize we're in a totally different area. It's not as if it's uninhabited, but there's more countryside, more greenery. I feel myself beginning to relax a little.

"We can put down the windows now," he says. "I don't like driving through the city with them down. Thank goodness for air conditioning."

"Hey, this is pretty out here," I say as he turns down a road that's bordered by a stretch of beach and palm trees. "Lots nicer than downtown."

"You haven't been out of the city yet?" he asks.

"No," Sid admits. "But we do have big plans for the weekend." Then she tells him about the Mount Hagen Sing-Sing. "And we just found out this is a once-a-year thing."

"You really got lucky in planning this trip."

"I like to think that God is watching out for us."

He doesn't respond to Sid's comment, but I sense by his silence that he's not too into God.

"We're going to a seaside restaurant tonight," he says as he pulls into an unpaved parking lot that merges onto the beach. "The reason we left early was so we could catch the sunset. I suppose you've already noticed how quickly the sun goes down this close to the equator."

"Yes," says Sid as we get out of the car. "We're from the North-west, where it doesn't go down until nine this time of year."

"Well, you can expect it to rise and set at six year round in this country."

I try to imagine what that would be like as we walk up a ramp that leads into a bamboo-sided building that's built on tall stilts and sits out over the water. So different from what I'm used to—so weird.

"This is a gorgeous location." Sid pauses to look at the water and palms and blue sky. "I feel like we've left the city far behind."

"Sometimes you need a break." He opens the door. "Especially in our line of work."

We go into a high-ceilinged, spacious room with the ever-present, slow-moving paddle fans overhead. Around the room are small tables with white tablecloths. One whole wall is wide open to the water and has a screened-in deck with more tables. Mr. Osterman speaks to one of the staff, and we're taken out to the deck and seated at a table along the edge.

"This is awesome," I tell him.

"Their food is awesome too," he says. "Let's go check it out."

Then he takes us over to a table where uncooked seafood and steaks are displayed on ice.

"Do they serve the food raw?" I ask quietly.

Mr. Osterman chuckles. "No, but they do let you pick out your entrée and tell them how you like it cooked."

"Cool."

He laughs. "Yes, cool for now, but nice and hot when they serve it."

Probably because I'm a farm girl at heart or possibly because I've had a lot of fish this past week, I go for the steak, medium rare. Then we quickly return to the table just in time to see the sun dipping down into clouds on the horizon of the ocean. The sky turns pink and coral and is very beautiful.

"I wish I'd brought a camera," says Sid.

I suddenly remember. "I did." I pull it out of my bag and hand it to Mr. Osterman, who takes a couple of shots of Sid and me with the gorgeous sunset behind us.

It's kind of a relief that we don't talk much about the AIDS crisis during dinner. I'm starting to feel a little overwhelmed and depressed by all that I've seen so far. I mean, it's cool what happened with Mary and Peter today, but at the same time, it's also sad. I think I want to escape. Of course, then I realize that people like Mary and Manoa and Pilada can't escape it, ever.

I try to distract myself by looking at the scenery outside. The water reflects the dying light in the sky, and a long canoe with a motor on the back slowly putters past. I wonder if they've been fishing. Sid and our host chat congenially, talking about people they discover they both know. Then he tells her how he got involved in USAID about twenty years ago, and she tells him a little about her career as a journalist. I don't pay too much attention; it's like I get to play the child for now. Sometimes it's nice to be a little oblivious.

After we finish an amazing meal, the best I've had since the Hawaiian luau, we're too stuffed to try any of the tempting dessert concoctions of tropical fruit, pastry, and cream. After we leave the restaurant and get back into the car, Mr. Osterman explains about the little tour he's going to give us on our way back to the hotel. "It's the seamy side of life in Port Moresby," he says, "but it will help you to get a visual of what's going on around here: the poverty, the conditions in general, and possibly why the AIDS epidemic seems to have no end in sight."

The car is quiet as he drives back toward the populated area. He takes a different route this time. We pass clusters of huts that are composed of a variety of materials, including pieces of scrap metal, cardboard, palm branches, and seemingly whatever was at hand. Dirty children and animals run about unsupervised, and the overall impression is one of extreme poverty and squalor. It's no wonder disease spreads so easily in this deprived environment.

"Clean water is a real problem around here," he says, "and there's no form of sanitation."

"Isn't that the situation all over this country?" asks Sid.

"Yes, but as you can imagine, it's greatly intensified in densely populated areas like this. Everyone is at a much higher risk here, not only for AIDS, but diseases like malaria, tuberculosis, and typhoid as well."

"It's sad that the things these people need are so basic," says Sid. "Water, food, medicine."

I can tell we're in the city limits now. Housing, if you can call it that, is denser, and people seem to be everywhere. I suppose I can't blame them for wanting to be outside when it's still so hot in the evening. Although I suppose they must be used to these temperatures.

"As we get closer to the city," he begins, "remember that we cannot stop the car or get out for any reason. We must keep the windows up and avoid direct eye contact with anyone who looks at the car." He clears his throat. "I must warn you it's quite likely you will see things that will upset and perhaps even repulse you tonight. And since I assume you're Christians, your instinct might be to get out and help. *Don't even think about it.* There's nothing you can do. You would only endanger everyone involved if you attempted such a thing. Is that perfectly clear?"

"Certainly," says Sid.

"Yes," I say quietly.

We drive by more clusters of housing. Men, women, children, and dogs mill about the streets, some sitting, some standing, some walking. But they all look a little lost. I wonder what makes them want to live here. And as we drive past, I can see they are looking at us. We're not the typical travelers through here. They probably think we are rich. Compared to them, we are.

"Why does anyone want to live here?" I ask.

"They come, thinking they'll find opportunity, jobs, a better life."

"But they don't?"

"Look around you," he says. "Does it look like it?"

"It looks like hell on earth to me," says Sid.

"Up ahead," he says, "that woman in the purple dress. Watch what's happening."

We look, and it's obvious she's a sex worker. Her clothing, for one thing, is a giveaway, and also we see a couple of men talking to her in a way that suggests it's not a normal conversation, especially in a country where men and women usually sit on opposite sides of a room. But then she sees our car and gets a hopeful look, like she thinks the driver may be looking for what she has to sell. She's clearly disappointed to discover he's not alone. At the same moment, one of the men grabs her by the hair, pulling her toward him in a suggestive way. The other man grabs her by the arms, and although she struggles, it's clear she is overpowered. I gasp at what I'm sure is about to happen.

"There's nothing we can do," says Mr. Osterman, almost as if reading my thoughts.

"I have my cell phone," says Sid. "Could we call the police?"

He laughs, but not in a happy way. "That's the last thing that woman needs."

"Yes," says Sid. "I've read of the corruption."

"They're trying to clamp down on it," he says, "but in cases like this, well, many policemen would be on the side of the woman's abusers."

"I assume women don't get a lot of respect here," says Sid.

"That's a huge part of this problem," he admits.

"Look at that," I say as I see a little girl being dragged behind a house by a man. She is kicking and screaming, but no one seems to notice.

"I'll bet that's not her father," says Sid angrily.

"Families don't tend to stick together in these parts," says Mr. Osterman. He sighs as if he is tired.

I feel tears coming down my cheeks now. I want to scream at him, to tell him this is enough. More than enough! He should *do* something. But he continues to drive through a more commercial section of town. There are signs suggesting all sorts of things that might be purchased inside the seedy-looking buildings. He points out more women who are obviously sex workers, along with more men who are obviously on the lookout for some action. The whole thing utterly disgusts me, and I actually get worried that I could throw up all over Mr. Osterman's tidy backseat. Finally he turns onto a street that seems a little more respectable.

"I'm sorry to shock you like that," he says, "but I figure if you want to be responsible journalists, you should see the whole picture. Ugly as it is."

"That was ugly," says Sid. She sounds as disgusted as I feel.

"Sickening," I add.

"Yes. Even though I've seen it a lot, I never get used to it. I hope I never will."

"What's the answer?" asks Sid as Mr. Osterman drives toward the center of town, which suddenly seems much cleaner than the first time I saw it.

"That's the sixty-four-thousand-dollar question," he says. "The sad thing is that it wasn't always like this. Back in the early eighties, this country seemed to be making real progress. There were improvements in health care. More schools were opening. Papua New Guinea's future seemed bright."

"What made it change? Was it just the Western influence?" Sid asks sadly. "I've heard that the Hollywood factor—movies and TV—has taken its toll on morality. And that alcoholism has skyrocketed due to persuasive marketing campaigns. I can't help but think this country was better off without those things."

"You know, that's an easy assumption and not entirely wrong. But it's more than that. I think you hit on it earlier when you commented on the treatment of women here. Historically speaking, women have not had a lot of respect. For generations, wife beating has been a perfectly acceptable practice."

"But what about the way they value their young women and charge a bride price for them?" I ask. "That would seem like they respect them a little."

"Think about it, Maddie," he says. "How would you feel if you could be sold to the highest bidder?"

91

"Yeah, I guess that wouldn't be too cool."

"Then take it a step further," he says. "What if your family sold you to the highest bidder and your new husband took you back to his village and beat you up? And then what if you went home to your family with broken bones and missing teeth and they got mad at you and told you to return to your husband?"

"I'd want to kill someone."

"But if you were the woman and you killed your abusive husband, even in self-defense, you would end up in jail, and depending on the jail, you could be in a worse situation there."

"Man, that's so unfair."

"So if you think about how women have been treated, how they've been devalued for hundreds of years, well, it all adds up to a real disaster." He pulls up in front of our hotel now. "I'm sorry if I depressed you nice ladies."

"That's okay," says Sid. "It was educational."

"And dinner was great," I add, although the niceness of dinner is lost on me now.

"You've got my card," he tells Sid. "Stay in touch."

"Thanks," she says. "I might have some more questions."

"And I'd like to see your article when it's finished."

She nods and closes the door, and then we slowly walk back into the hotel. I can tell that we're both dragging now. It's like our little tour has totally bummed us out.

"Sorry about that," Sid tells me as we walk through the lobby.

"It's not your fault."

"I shouldn't have taken you tonight."

"Why not?"

"For one thing, it was dangerous driving through that part of town at night."

"Yeah, maybe. But you don't think Mr. Osterman would have taken us someplace where we were in real danger, do you?"

"I think he's become a little callous to some of this."

"What a horrible job," I say as I push the elevator button.

"I'm sure it gets depressing. However, he does seem to really care about the country, and I think he does a good job of allocating funding to helpful programs. Still, it can't be easy, especially for someone without faith."

I'm thinking it's depressing for someone *with* faith. I mean, where is God when all this is happening? Can't he do something? Why do these people have to suffer so much? Just because they're poor? It all seems so wrong. So totally wrong!

NINE

O nce again we're awakened by an early morning phone call. It's a little past seven when Sid picks it up.

"Sure, that would be great, Peter," she says sleepily. "Yes, we can easily be ready by ten. Thank you so much."

She hangs up the phone and turns to me. "Peter expects to finish up at the printers before ten, and Lydia suggested he take us to see how AIDS patients are treated in the city hospital, which isn't too far from here." She shakes her head. "From what I've heard from Dr. Larson, we shouldn't expect much."

So we get our showers, then head downstairs for breakfast.

"Dr. Larson said that the city hospital has an AIDS ward, but they're not allowed to call it that."

"Why not?"

"The stigma. Apparently they'd have no patients if it was labeled the AIDS ward. People don't like to admit they really do have AIDS."

I nod. "Yes, I got a taste of that yesterday. So sad."

We finish breakfast and go to the lobby to wait for Peter. He seems to be in a cheerful mood, humming as he drives us through town. I'm not sure if this is because of his positive experience helping the AIDS patients yesterday or because he's simply eager to go home today. Maybe a combination of both.

"I have something for you," he says as he parks in a lot by the large hospital. "To help you to understand pidgin."

As we get out of the car, he gives us both little booklets that say *Tok Pisin* on the front.

"What does *Tok Pisin* mean?" I ask.

"*Tok* means 'language.' *Tok Pisin* is 'pidgin English' or 'Neo-Melanesian.' *Tok ples* means 'the language of your people.' Your tok ples is English. My tok ples is Lomokakon."

"Oh."

"Maybe you will have time to learn some words as we travel today."

"Thank you," says Sid. "This will be helpful."

"Lydia said we must go to Ward 3B," announces Peter as we come to the entrance of the hospital.

Once inside, Sid asks for directions. The receptionist gives us a slightly perplexed look but tells us how to find the ward. I immediately get the feeling that this hospital isn't nearly as clean or orderly as Saint Luke's. But it gets far worse when we reach Ward 3B.

"Look," says Sid in a quiet tone, nodding to a brown box at the nurses' station next to the Ward 3B entrance. On the side of this cardboard box, handwritten in black, bold letters, are the words "Death Certificates." Inside I see a stack of official-looking forms all ready to be used, as if they need to keep these documents handy. Chilling.

Sid talks to an English-speaking nurse, and the woman nods, but her expression is apathetic. "Feel free to have a look," she says in a flat

British accent, turning back to a clipboard where she's writing something down.

We walk into Ward 3B, and I'm instantly hit by the stench, followed by a strong wave of nausea. Malarone or not, I think this place could make anyone feel sick. I notice that Peter has a mixture of disgust and dismay on his face, and Sid looks totally appalled. I see bedpans that need emptying and all sorts of medical garbage just lying around. It's as if no one really cares. And the expressions on the patients' faces convey nothing but dejection and hopelessness. I'm not sure I can handle this. But I remind myself of what my dad likes to say to me when I'm faced with a particularly gross task in the barn. "Buck up, Maddie. Get in, get it over with, get out."

I'm startled to see a woman wearing street clothes curled up on the floor beneath a hospital bed. Her head is resting on a small blue suitcase. The man in the bed above her looks half-dead. The woman doesn't look much better.

"Hello," says a short Asian man in a white medical jacket. "I'm Dr. Sing. This is my floor. Can I help you?"

Sid quickly explains why we're here, and Dr. Sing does not look the least bit pleased.

"This is *not* an AIDS ward," he's quick to point out.

"But the patients here do have AIDS?" persists Sid.

"Some of them are being treated for HIV/AIDS."

"Is this ward typical of the conditions in the rest of this hospital?" she asks.

He frowns. "These people would be on the street if they weren't here. We do what we can to help. They are all terminal."

"I'm not here to criticize your facility," says Sid in a gentler tone. "If anything, I hope that telling the world what's going on in this country, the proportions of this epidemic, will help to change things."

A tiny flicker of interest crosses his face. "We do need more funding, more medicine, more and better-trained health workers."

She nods. "Yes, we can see that."

Then he frowns again. "But no one seems to listen to our cry."

"And you need better AIDS-awareness education," she adds.

"Yes, of course. But it's not easy. It's never easy." He glances over his shoulder. "I'm sorry, but I have calls to make."

"Thank you for your time, Doctor."

He bows slightly and leaves the ward.

Sid looks down at the woman on the floor now. We seem to have disturbed her, and she slowly scoots out from beneath the bed. She looks at us warily as she slips her bare feet into worn rubber flip-flops.

"Please, Peter, ask the woman why she was sleeping under the bed," Sid says quickly.

Peter speaks to the woman in a kind voice, and although she seems embarrassed, she does answer him.

"She says the man in the bed is her husband, and she is here to take care of him."

"Ask her if she's willing to talk to us," says Sid. "Tell her we will pay her for her time if she will answer some questions."

Peter speaks to her again, and her countenance instantly changes. She is smiling and nodding now. Happy, it seems, to earn some money. Not surprising, since I've heard the average daily wage in this country equals about a dollar.

"Ask her if she would mind leaving the ward so we can go somewhere else to sit down and talk," says Sid.

Peter speaks to her again, and she peers closely at the motionless man, putting her head close to his face, maybe to determine if he's breathing. Satisfied, she says something to Peter and nods at us.

"Her name is Abu Piliki," he tells us. "Her village is on the coast, about thirty kilometers north of Port Moresby."

I'm so relieved to leave this ward behind. I was trying to be strong, but I don't think I've ever seen or smelled anything so disgustingly horrible—far worse than the smells of farm animals. I ask Sid if there's a place we could sit outside to talk, and she tells me to go find out. So I hurry over to the nurses' station and ask the British nurse with the clipboard. She gives me some quick directions, and I take our little group down the elevator to the first floor and then on to the cafeteria, where I spot a small terrace off to one side.

"Ask Abu if she's hungry," Sid says to Peter as we enter the cafeteria.

Peter asks, and she nods eagerly. So we get her some food and some tea for Peter and soft drinks for Sid and me, then we go outside, where I feel like I can breathe again. I inhale deeply, hoping to rid my lungs of the foul air that has filled them. Sure, there is diesel exhaust as well as city smells out here, but it's so much better than Ward 3B.

Sid waits for Abu to eat, which she does quickly. Then Sid begins to question her, starting with why she was sleeping under her husband's bed just now. Through Peter, Abu explains that family members must leave their homes to come and care for patients. It seems the hospital doesn't have enough workers, so without family to fill in the gap, patients would suffer even more.

"She says her husband will starve if she does not bring him food each day," Peter tells us.

"Doesn't the hospital provide food?" I ask.

He translates, and she shakes her head, holding up her hands dramatically as she says, "Nogat, nogat!" which I know means "no."

"Ask her if her husband has AIDS," says Sid. I just naturally assumed that was the case, but I realize it hasn't been brought up.

Abu seems reluctant to answer at first, but Peter presses her, and finally she admits that he does indeed have AIDS. Peter asks her another question, and now she seems even more embarrassed. She looks away. But he asks her again, and then she nods.

"She has AIDS too," he tells us.

"Ask her why she is so embarrassed to tell us this," says Sid.

Peter speaks to her in a very gentle tone now, and although she looks uncomfortable, she finally begins to speak. As she does, Peter translates.

"She has seen people beaten to death or even buried alive in her village," he says, "just because they had AIDS. It is a sickness that brings great shame. Many believe the sickness comes from evil spirits and that people who get AIDS are being punished for bad deeds." He looks at me now. "Remember what I told you yesterday? I believed AIDS was evil too." He looks down at his empty teacup, then back up at us. "I do not believe that now."

We also find out that Abu has two small children. Her mother is taking care of them. No one in her village knows that her husband is being treated for AIDS. They think he has hepatitis. She has not had her children tested for AIDS. Sid asks why not, and Abu tells us she is afraid. They are too young. What would she do if they tested positive? She can't afford medicine.

Finally Sid seems satisfied, and she pays Abu twenty kina for talking to us. Abu clutches the money, tears streaming down her face as she thanks us over and over. Then she says she must return to her husband. But before she goes, I ask Peter if I can ask her one more question, and she agrees.

"Ask Abu if she loves her husband," I say, and Peter looks slightly surprised by this.

"What kind of love do you mean?" he asks me.

Okay, now I'm not sure how to explain what seems an obvious question, and my hesitation seems to embarrass him a bit.

"Do you mean respectful love?" he asks, to clarify.

"Yes," I say quickly, grateful for any help.

So he asks Abu this final question, and now she seems just as stumped as Peter was. Finally she speaks, slowly, as if she's carefully considering each word. Peter nods as if he understands her meaning, and then he translates for us. "She says her husband is a good man. He has been good to her and their two young sons. When he was well, he was a fisherman. He does not beat her. She is sorry he is sick. She will be sad if he dies."

"Thank you," I say to both Peter and Abu.

Abu thanks us again, then leaves.

"I shouldn't have asked her that," I admit as soon as Abu has gone back into the cafeteria. "I'm sorry."

"It was an excellent question," Sid assures me. "I wish I'd thought to ask it myself."

"Really?"

"It was a *hard* question," says Peter.

"Why is that?" asks Sid.

"In pidgin English the only word for 'love' is *bel i gut.*"

"And what exactly does that mean?" persists Sid.

"It means 'a good feeling in the belly.'"

I consider this. "That's kind of like love, a good feeling inside."

"Yes, in pidgin, bel i gut is used for all kinds of love. But it does not say everything." He pauses as if thinking of a way to explain. "In my tok ples, my tribal language, there are many words for love," he continues. "There is love for parents, which is like respect and honor. There is love for children, which is like caring for them. There is love for brothers and sisters, which is the same as love for a friend. And love for things like good food or a beautiful bird—that word means to take delight in something, like laughter."

"What about the word for love between husbands and wives?" asks Sid. "Is there a word for that?"

"There is the word for, uh, 'copulation,'" he says, looking aside as if he is uncomfortable.

"But not another word for love?" persists Sid. "What about love for God? Is there a word for that?"

His eyes light up now. "No, there is no tok ples word for that kind of love either. That was a problem in my translation work with the

Johnsons. We used a few tribal words to make the meaning of God's love clear."

"What about your wife?" I ask Peter. "Do you love her?"

He smiles. "Oh yes. Very much."

"But you don't have a word for that kind of love. What would you say to her?"

He looks embarrassed again. "Oh, we do not speak like that to one another. Not with words. But I know that it is right. I know the Bible says, husband, love your wife."

"And you do that?" I ask.

"Yes." His eyes light up. "I do that."

"Your wife is a blessed woman," I tell him.

"I am a blessed man."

Just for the sake of contrast, we decide to check out some of the other wards in this hospital. We want to see how they compare to Ward 3B. And while I wouldn't care to be hospitalized in any of them, none have the extremely impoverished conditions of the AIDS ward.

"They can call Ward 3B whatever they like," says Sid as we're leaving, "but it is definitely the AIDS ward, and patients with AIDS are definitely treated with much less care and respect than the others."

"They are treated like lepers," says Peter.

"Exactly," I agree.

"But Jesus healed the leper," Peter says as he unlocks the car and opens the passenger door for Sid.

"I wish we could too," I say.

"Maybe we should pray for them," says Peter earnestly, "pray that they would take up their beds and walk!"

103

"Maybe we should," I say, although I'm uncertain. I mean I've already been praying for the people we've met. But to pray for them to be physically healed? I don't know if I have that kind of faith. And, okay, that seriously bugs me.

TEN

I think we should check out of this hotel," says Sid as we go up to
our room.

"Check out?" I repeat. "Is something wrong?"

"No, I just think it's time to see more of the country. To write a
complete story on New Guinea and its problems, I need to see the
bigger picture, and that must extend beyond Port Moresby."

"You mean we won't come back here after we see Mount Hagen?"

"Exactly. I'd like to get a flight to another part of the country.
I want to see how the AIDS epidemic is being handled in a less-
populated area."

I nod. "That makes sense."

"So are you game for some adventure?"

"Sure, why not?"

"We can always come back here if it doesn't work out," she says
as we go into our room. "But, for now, let's pack everything up and
check out."

So we pack up and carry our luggage downstairs. Sid checks us
out, and we eat a quick lunch in the hotel restaurant. Just as we finish, Peter arrives.

"All ready for the big trip?" he asks.

Sid points to our luggage that's sitting next to the concierge desk. His eyes grow wide. "You're taking all that?"

Sid explains our plan to travel on after the weekend, but Peter still looks a bit concerned. Still, he helps us load our suitcases into the trunk. Then we go to pick up Lydia. Unlike us, she is traveling light. She has only a small duffel bag and her purse. And when she puts the duffel bag in back, she, too, looks concerned.

"That's a lot of luggage," she says to Sid.

Once again Sid explains our plan.

When we get to the airport, we begin to understand their concern. It turns out that we're flying in a small Cessna plane, and there is a weight limit. Sid learns that our tickets will be charged by the pound, which means that our luggage must be weighed and paid for accordingly. And after it's weighed, we're invited to step on the scales as well. Okay, this is a little embarrassing, but knowing it's a safety issue, I cooperate.

"The air gets thinner in the highlands," explains Jim, the pilot. "We need to be careful not to overload the plane. It's too taxing on the engine."

"How are we doing as far as weight goes?" asks Sid as he punches some numbers into his calculator and waits for the results.

"We're okay," he finally says. Then he tells her how much the flight will cost, and to our surprise, it's not too bad.

We're loaded into the plane, and before long we're taking off. This is the first time I've flown in a small plane. Will I ever overcome my fear of flying?

The sound of the engine is loud as we gain enough altitude to assure me that we're not going to get caught in the tall treetops below us. I'm amazed at how they resemble overgrown broccoli stalks. I realize I'm holding my breath as I look out the window, and I force myself to exhale as I watch everything below us getting smaller. Soon we're out of the city limits, and it looks like nothing but vegetation below— not exactly the sort of terrain you'd pick for an emergency landing. Not that we're going to do that.

Occasionally I spy a brown circle of earth and small round structures peppered about, which I assume are little houses or huts that are part of a village. Sid is sitting up front, next to the pilot, and I can hear him pointing out some sight to her, like a river or something, but the engine's so noisy that I can't really make out what he's saying. I just hope he's focusing on his flying and the instrument panel in front of him.

"It's only a short flight," shouts Lydia, who's sitting beside me. She smiles at me as if she can tell that I'm nervous. "And JAARS pilots are the best in the world." The plane levels out now, and the roar of the engine diminishes so that I can hear.

"What are 'jars' pilots?" I ask, imagining pilots who fly around in glass bottles.

"It stands for Jungle Aviation and Radio Service," she tells me. "They provide technical support for SIL."

I have to think for a moment before I remember that SIL is Summer Institute of Linguistics, the translation organization her adoptive parents work for. Still, I don't really understand the meaning of the name. "Summer Institute of Linguistics sounds like a school to me," I say. "But didn't you say your parents are Bible translators?"

She smiles. "Yes, it's confusing to many people. SIL is about linguistic and translation work. The organization is related to Wycliffe Bible Translators."

"Oh, I have heard of Wycliffe," I tell her. "I think someone from there spoke at our church once."

"I wouldn't be surprised," she says. "My parents go to the States every six years for deputation."

"What's that?"

"It's the way they earn their support. All the translators are self-supported—'faith missionaries.' They can't come into the country to translate without all their financial donations lined up."

"Oh."

"I used to feel embarrassed when we went around from church to church," she tells me. "It felt like begging to me. But then I began to understand that people who aren't able to go out and be missionaries really like to partner with those who can. Now I don't feel bad anymore."

"That makes sense," I say.

Peter is sitting in the small single seat in the back, but he must be listening to us. "I went to the United States with the Johnsons for one month last time," he tells me. "I got to speak in the churches too. I told the American people how important translation work is in my country."

"And he did an excellent job," adds Lydia. "Giving really went up."

"What did you think of America?" I ask, turning around to see Peter's face.

His eyes grow wide as he shakes his head. "It was very, very strange."

"I remember the first time we took him to a Wal-Mart Supercenter," says Lydia, suppressing laughter. "It was as if we had landed on the moon."

"Too many things," he says, "all in one place."

"I have to admit that I get overwhelmed too," she says.

"Don't feel bad," I tell her. "So do I."

"Really?" She seems surprised. "I thought Americans were used to all that."

"Well, I grew up in a rural area," I admit. "My parents are farmers."

"Farmers?" says Peter from behind me. "Truly?"

So I tell them a little about my family's farm, explaining about caring for our livestock and the crops we grow and how everyone in my family helps out. And both Lydia and Peter seem surprised.

"I guess we spend so much time in big cities," says Lydia, "that we begin to think all Americans live like that."

"Not me." I grin at her.

"We'll be landing in Aiyura in about fifteen minutes," says Jim.

"Aiyura?" I repeat, glancing at Lydia. "I thought we were going to Mount Hagen."

"Aiyura is the JAARS landing strip," she explains. "It's in Ukarumpa."

"Ukarumpa?" I let the strange word bounce off my tongue.

"Yes, that's SIL's mission base."

"What does that mean exactly?"

"Well, oddly enough, it's like a tiny American city."

"Huh?" Now I'm sorry, but this just sounds weird. A tiny American city way out here in the middle of nowhere. I wonder if they have a Starbucks.

"I guess you'll have to see it to understand." She laughs. "It seemed more like a city after I'd been in our village for a long time. For you it will probably just seem like a small American town."

I look out the window to see jagged, tree-covered mountains with patches of white clouds filling the crevices. The terrain looks rugged and foreboding, and it's hard to imagine how there could be a safe, flat place to land anywhere at this elevation. But before long the plane begins to descend, and I see a green field with what must be a landing strip cutting through the center. Before I know it, we're landing. After the plane is solidly on the ground, I remember to breathe again.

"We made it," says Lydia.

Jim taxis the plane over to a small metal building, and a couple of New Guinean men come over and wait for us to get out.

Peter hugs the men, and they both warmly greet Lydia. The taller one, introduced as Michael, has been sent by her parents to give us a ride to their village. The other one is an old friend who's been doing some translation checking here in Ukarumpa.

Lydia explains that her village is between Ukarumpa and Mount Hagen and that it will take us about two hours to drive there.

"Is it safe to drive these roads?" asks Sid as they load our things into the back of a beat-up yellow Land Rover.

"Depends on how you define *safe*," I say, remembering what Lydia told me the other day. I wink at Lydia.

"God will watch over us." Lydia tosses her duffel bag in. "He always does."

"We should be in Lomokako before sundown," Michael tells us as he starts the engine. He and Peter are in front, and Sid and Lydia and I are in back.

"I'd like to see Ukarumpa sometime," I say as he begins to drive.

"Perhaps you can schedule time here before you go to your next stop," suggests Lydia.

"Do you think it will be difficult to get a flight somewhere after the weekend?" Sid asks.

"It could be tricky to get out of Mount Hagen right after the big sing-sing," says Lydia. "It's a fairly large tourist attraction that draws people from all over the world. But my parents could radio JAARS and see what flights are available for next week. Do you know where you want to go?"

Sid laughs. "That's just it. We don't know. Maybe your parents will have some recommendations."

I'm surprised Lydia is able to sleep as we drive along the uneven and curvy mountain road. But her head is back, and she appears to be resting soundly. Consequently, Sid and I, on either side of her, remain quiet as we look out our windows. I wish I'd known I was going to be on the cliff side. I feel my heart jumping into my throat again and again as we careen around sharp corners that seem to drop off into nowhere. At times I'm not even sure all four tires are on the road. In the front seat, Michael and Peter chatter away obliviously. I'm guessing they're using their tribal language, because I'm not hearing words like *long* or *tumus* or *laik,* which seem to pop up in almost every sentence in pidgin. This reminds me of the little blue *Tok Pisin* booklet that Peter gave us. I dig it out of my purse, and in hopes of distracting myself from a heart attack, I attempt to read it, starting with the pronunciation guide, which seems fairly straightforward.

There are only two prepositions: *bilong* (pronounced *belong*), which means "of" or "for," and *long,* which means everything else. That explains why I hear that word so much. *Yu* means "you," and *mi* means "me." But you can combine them to include others by saying *yupela,* which is like "you guys," or *mipela,* which is like "us." At least I think that's what it means. Verbs are simple. *Go* means "go." *Stap* means "stay." So I'm trying to put together my first pidgin sentence, in my head anyway, since I'm not ready to try it out loud just yet. *Mi go.* Okay, that's pretty basic, but it's a start. *Yumi go.* I study a list of commonly used words and see if I can string something together that sounds a bit more intelligent.

bagarap(im)—broken, to break down
balus—airplane
bikpela—big
haus—house
kaikai—food, eat
kamap—arrive, become
kisim—get
man—man
manmeri—people
meri—woman

Papa God—God
pikinini—child
raus(im)—get out
sapos(im)—if
save—know
slip—sleep, live
stap(im)—be, stay
tasol—only

Finally I come up with something. I practice it in my head a few times, hoping that I've got it right and that I'll be able to say it when we arrive in Lydia's village. This is it: *Mi stap long haus bilong Lydia.* This should mean "I will stay at Lydia's house." At least I hope so. I try some more. *Yumi slip long haus bilong Lydia.* That should mean "We will sleep at Lydia's house." And I think if I replace *slip* with *kaikaim,* it means we'll eat at Lydia's house. At least I hope we'll eat. I'm already starting to get hungry.

It feels like we've been driving forever, but finally the Land Rover slows down, and I'm thinking maybe we're there. But when I look up, I notice four men standing on the road, and the expressions on their faces do not look good. My heart starts to race, and I immediately envision the possibility of a carjacking, a kidnapping, possibly even a rape. All this flashes through my mind faster than the speed of light. And I suddenly feel the reality of how far we are out in the middle of nowhere. Literally the ends of the earth. I'm fairly certain Sid's cell phone won't work up here.

Peter puts his window down a bit and yells something at the men.

They yell back, shaking fists and sticks. Then Michael puts down his window partway and yells something. Again they yell back. By now Lydia has jerked awake, and she looks out to see what's going on. At first she seems frightened too, but then she closes her eyes, and her lips begin to move, and I'm sure she's praying. I see Sid following her lead, so I close my eyes and pray too.

Then the Land Rover is moving again. Michael steps so hard on the gas that our heads whip back, but when I look to see what's happening, we are whizzing past the four angry men. I hear a loud thud as one of the sticks whacks the back of the vehicle.

"Sorry about that," says Lydia, leaning back with a sigh. "But we'll soon be home."

"Who were those men?" asks Sid.

"They were from another village," says Lydia. "Not a friendly village either."

"That seemed obvious."

"What were they saying to you, Peter?" asks Sid.

"They wanted the car," he tells us.

"To steal it?" asks Sid.

"Yes." His tone is weary. "They are fools."

"Well, I'm glad you didn't give the car to them," I say. This makes Michael and Peter laugh.

"No," says Peter. "Just because they ask does not mean we must give."

I think about how Jesus said to give a man your coat when he asks for your shirt, but I have no idea how that would apply in this situation. Mostly I am hugely relieved that Michael and Peter didn't give them the Land Rover.

"Hey, I learned some pidgin while you were asleep," I tell Lydia, eager for something to change the subject.

"You did?"

"Yes, let me see if I can remember. Okay. Mi stap long haus bilong Lydia."

She claps her hands. "Very good!"

"What does it mean?" demands my aunt.

"I will stay at Lydia's house," I proclaim.

Sid insists I teach it to her, and then Lydia steps in and teaches us some more simple sentences. We learn to ask for directions and how much something costs and lots of little things. I just hope I can remember them.

"Pidgin is a lot easier than I thought," says Sid as she studies her *Tok Pisin* booklet.

"Yes," says Lydia. "If you can get people to speak slowly and clearly, it's not too hard. The problem is that they get going too fast, and you'll probably get lost."

"It is the same in your country," says Peter from the front seat. "I speak good English, but people talk too fast, and I am lost."

"But we're not lost now," says Lydia, happily pointing off to the right. "There is our village, right down this road. Welcome to Lomokako!" Michael turns off the main road onto a narrow dirt road that leads through some tall trees. It finally opens up into an area of packed dirt that's a bit smaller than the infield of a baseball diamond. Around

MELODY CARLSON

the perimeters of this area are small, roundish, brown houses with palm-thatched roofs that have narrow plumes of smoke coming out of the centers. The houses are built slightly off the ground with doors that face the open area, where children and animals are playing. Diverted by our arrival, most of the children run over to see who has come.

I notice how the women, sitting in front of the open doorways, look up at us. They appear to be working on things. Perhaps their evening meals or maybe some kind of handiwork, but they all smile and wave. Some stand and come over, shooing the children back as the Land Rover parks by a brown structure that's set slightly back and is much larger and squarer than the others.

"We are home!" says Lydia.

ELEVEN

The first thing I notice as we get out of the Land Rover is that it's colder up here. I take a deep breath and feel a sense of relief that we're at a much higher elevation than Port Moresby. The air not only feels cooler but cleaner, and it seems the vegetation is different. I like it.

An older couple comes out to greet us, and I assume these are Lydia's parents because they both immediately embrace her. Introductions are made, then we gather our things and follow the Johnsons to the largest wooden building, which turns out to be their house. In a way, the Johnsons remind me of my own parents. They're about the same age as mine and are just regular-looking folks who seem genuinely friendly. To my surprised relief, I feel unexpectedly at home with them.

"How was the trip?" asks Mrs. Johnson as she takes a bag from Sid.

"Very interesting," says my aunt. "Quite an experience."

Peter quickly relays our encounter with the violent men on the road, and Mr. Johnson just shakes his head. "It's probably because of the Mount Hagen Sing-Sing," he says as he opens a wooden door to the screened porch that wraps around the front part of their house.

"Things can get a little crazy during these celebrations. Some people think it's a good excuse for a free-for-all."

"Or a time to settle old differences," adds Mrs. Johnson.

"What sort of differences?" asks Sid.

"Oh, the usual things," says Mr. Johnson. "Thievery, trickery, marital disputes."

"Sometimes it's just an old payback," says Mrs. Johnson. "Have you heard about paybacks yet?"

"No," says Sid. "What's a payback?"

"It's the old tribal way of getting retribution," says Mrs. Johnson. "For instance, if someone from a neighboring tribe accidentally ran over your pig, a payback would be running over their pig to get even."

"The old eye for an eye, tooth for a tooth," adds Mr. Johnson.

"But travelers need to be aware of this practice," says Mrs. Johnson. "If you're ever involved in an accident, the safest thing is to leave the scene immediately."

"Wouldn't that be a hit-and-run?" I ask.

"Not in these parts," says Lydia. "When you reached the next town, you'd simply inform the police of what had happened."

"That's right," says her dad. "If you stick around, you could be in real danger of retribution."

"Come inside, come inside," says Mrs. Johnson, opening the door into the house. "We don't need to dwell on such dismal topics before you're even in the front door."

"It's okay," says Sid. "It's very interesting."

"Well, we certainly don't want to scare you," says Mr. Johnson. "It's really not all that bad. And as far as the sing-sing goes, you should know that there are plenty of security guards around here this time of year. They're supposed to be ready for these little problems."

Lydia laughs, as if her dad's comment isn't meant to be taken too seriously. Then she shows us to a small bedroom that we'll share. "It's my brothers' room," she explains. "Sorry about the bunk beds, but it's to conserve space."

"It's just fine," says Sid as she sets her bag on a chair.

"We can flip for the top bunk," I add.

"I'll concede it to you," she says.

"Why are there bars on the windows?" I ask. "I mean, I realize that's the norm in the city, but is it really that unsafe out here too?"

"We've had problems," Lydia tells us. "Dad put them up about ten years ago. At first we kids hated it. We thought we were in prison. But after a while we got used to it, and now we hardly even notice them."

"Supper will be ready in about twenty minutes," calls Mrs. Johnson.

"The bathroom is this way," says Lydia, taking us around a corner to the back and into a fairly normal-looking bathroom.

"And you have running water too," observes Sid.

"It's from a well that was dug long before I was born."

"Does it serve the whole village?"

"Yes. My parents say there was a lot more illness here before the well went in. Just one of the many benefits for villages with missionaries living in their midst."

"Do the villagers appreciate that?" I ask. I'm curious, because it seems there are a lot of nationals unhappy about life in general.

"Oh yes," says Lydia. "I think almost everyone here loves my parents and our family."

"Almost?" I question.

She smiles. "Oh, you know what they say about pleasing all the people all the time."

"Not possible," says Sid.

"Right." Lydia points to a toilet against the back wall. "And we actually have a flushing toilet too," she explains. "It may seem like no big deal to most Americans, but my family was so happy when it was installed. Some friends of my parents came to visit when we were kids. Their church sent them to put in a septic system for our house."

"Very modern," says Sid.

"Yes," I agree. "Swanky."

Lydia laughs. "Now that's one I haven't heard before. But the truth is, many missionaries still rely on outhouses." She points to the shower area, which also looks fairly normal, except there is a bucket with a nozzle on it hanging from a rafter in the high ceiling. "I'll warn you about our hot-water system. For the most part, we rely on a solar unit, but during a cloudy spell, it can get a little chilly. So we sometimes use the bucket shower with hot water from the cookstove. You may have to do that while you're here."

"I've had bucket showers before," says Sid, "and it's not too bad once you get the hang of it."

I notice something long and green scampering atop one of the open beams that run below the high, vaulted ceiling. "What's that?" I ask.

"Just a gecko," she says. "They're good to have around."

"He's cute," I say, going closer for a better look.

"And harmless. Sort of a natural pesticide since they eat bugs."

Sid points up to the ceiling, which is ridged and painted white. "Is that the corrugated metal roof that we saw from outside?"

Lydia nods. "My brothers helped my dad put that on one year. Before they installed the sheets, Mom and I painted the interior side white. She thought it would reflect more light, which it does. Before that, our house had a thatched palm roof like the rest of the village, and all kinds of things like to live in those roofs. Mom was so happy when we got rid of it. The house stays a lot cleaner. The metal roof also allowed my dad to set up a system to save rainwater for use in our house. It makes more well water available to the village."

"Very efficient," says Sid. "Americans should come over here and learn a few things."

"I doubt most Americans would want to be bothered with the extra work it takes to live like this," says Lydia. "At least that's the impression I got while I was there. It seems everyone likes things fast and easy."

I consider this as Lydia gives us the rest of the tour. Although her house is not very large, it seems to have a smart design, and much of it is open, which probably makes it seem bigger than it is. You can tell her parents have put a lot of thought into it.

"What are the floors made of?" I ask. "They feel kind of springy."

"That's bamboo," she says. "Just split and laid out like sticks. Not the greatest thing for bare feet, since you can get splinters, but it's tough. And cheap."

"I really like your house," I tell Mrs. Johnson when we stop in the kitchen. "It's very homey."

"Thanks. It seems to suit us." She's stirring the contents of a large cast-iron pot on the big wood-burning cookstove.

"I'm surprised this stove doesn't make it too hot in here," I say as I feel the heat radiating from it.

"Sometimes it does," she admits. "And then I have to open all the windows and get a breeze going through. Or else I'll try to do most of the cooking earlier in the day. But this is our cool season, and it's been extra chilly lately."

"I noticed the temperature change when we got here," I say. "But it feels good to me. I guess I'm not much of a hot-climate person."

"I'm not either." Mrs. Johnson sets the spoon down. "Where are you from?"

I tell her that Sid and I are from Washington, and she smiles. "You see, I thought we had something in common. We're from Portland, Oregon. Practically neighbors."

Lydia helps her mother in the kitchen as if she's done this a thousand times before. The same way I would be doing it if I was at home with my mom. Still, this scene catches me slightly off guard. Mrs. Johnson is very fair with blond hair that's fading to silver. In contrast, Lydia's bronze-colored skin and dark, curly hair look very much like the New Guinean girl that she is. And yet they seem to fit together perfectly.

Soon dinner is ready, and we all sit together at a long wooden table that separates the kitchen from the sitting area. It looks handmade from large pieces of wood and appears to have hosted a generation's worth of family meals. Mr. Johnson bows his head and says a prayer, and we begin to eat.

"I hope you like spaghetti with tomato and meat sauce," says Mrs. Johnson as she passes a big bowl of pasta around.

"I feel like I'm home," I say happily. "This is just the way my mom makes spaghetti."

"And garlic bread," says Lydia. "My favorite!"

"This could end up being the best meal we've had in Papua New Guinea," I tell them.

"That's true," says Sid. "And we had a very nice dinner just outside of Port Moresby." Then she describes the fancy seaside restaurant, which the Johnsons have heard of but haven't been able to afford.

Of course, this reminds me of the horrible tour we had afterward, and I think tonight's meal isn't only better but will be much more digestible too.

"How do you get electricity?" I ask, noticing that besides the pretty kerosene lantern in the center of the table, there's an electric overhead light in the kitchen as well.

"We have a diesel generator," says Mr. Johnson. "We try not to use it for too much. A few lights, the computer, music—that's about it."

"The TV and VCR," Lydia reminds him.

He laughs. "Yes. When the kids were at home, the generator was well used for playing all the videos that people back home sent to us. Sometimes I even made the kids work to earn money to pay for the extra diesel."

"Yes, you were so hard on us, Dad," teases Lydia.

"What a way to grow up," says Sid, "living out here at what seems the end of the earth to the rest of us. What was it like for you and your brothers, Lydia?"

Mrs. Johnson laughs. "That's probably a question you shouldn't ask with her parents present."

"No, it's okay," says Lydia thoughtfully. "It was a good way to grow up. God has blessed me with such a wonderful family." She smiles at her parents. "We're not perfect. We all know that. But I could not imagine better parents."

"And we couldn't have been blessed with a better daughter," says Mrs. Johnson. "We will never stop giving thanks for our little Lydia." But as she pats Lydia's hand, I think I see a trace of sadness in her eyes. Perhaps it's just that old parental thing about watching your kids grow up. But it's definitely there.

"But we have others to thank too," says Mr. Johnson. "A lot of people had a hand in raising our kids."

"How's that?" I ask.

"Well, we homeschooled them out here in the village for quite a while. But when they got to be teenagers, they wanted to go to the base for school."

"Ukarumpa?" says Sid.

"Yes. They have a very fine high school there. And it's a good way for kids to have a social life that better prepares them for the world at large."

"Or so we hoped," says Mrs. Johnson.

Mr. Johnson clears his throat. "Yes. I don't mean to pretend that the mission-base school doesn't have its problems. What high school doesn't?"

"Are you saying that missionary children get into trouble?" asks Sid.

He nods. "Most certainly. Some of them get into quite a bit of trouble."

"Oh, Jeremy and Caleb weren't that bad, Dad," says Lydia.

"No, they weren't. But they did sow some wild oats, I'm afraid."

"At least they didn't go to jail," says Lydia.

"Thank the Lord," says Mrs. Johnson. "We can't say that for all the missionary kids."

"Wow," I say. "That surprises me."

"Why?" asks Lydia. "We're not so different from you."

I sort of laugh. "Well, I know that. But I guess I assumed that having been raised by strong Christian parents...well...you know." I pause, considering my words. "You seem pretty mature and responsible. More so than most of my friends back home, and they're all about your age."

She smiles. "Thank you."

"Lydia is exceptional," says Mr. Johnson. "We think she was born old and wise."

Mrs. Johnson nods. "Yes. She was a surprising child. Right from the start. She had these two older brothers to chase after, and it wasn't long before she caught up to them in their studies."

"We understand that Lydia wants to go to med school," says Sid.

The room gets quiet now, and I wonder if I overstepped a boundary by sharing this information with my aunt.

"Yes," says Lydia in a slightly self-conscious way. "I told Maddie about my dream to be a doctor."

"It's a big dream," says her dad.

"But not an impossible one," says Sid.

Mrs. Johnson frowns as she begins to clear the table. I can tell this isn't a subject she's comfortable with. Lydia hops up and helps her mother, and I offer to help too, but they both say no.

"I was wondering," says Sid to Mr. Johnson, "how you would feel if we were to set up a scholarship fund for Lydia."

"That's very kind and generous of you," he says, glancing over our heads to where Lydia and her mom are working in the kitchen. But his expression is troubled now, as if this isn't a comfortable subject for any of them. "Perhaps we can discuss this later."

"Of course," says Sid apologetically. "I shouldn't have brought it up at dinner like this. Please, forgive me."

He waves his hand. "Not a problem."

"And we have dessert," announces Lydia. "Mom made an apple pie."

"No way!" I say. "Apple pie? That doesn't seem possible. Where do you get apples in New Guinea?"

"We actually have some species that grow in the highlands," Mrs. Johnson says as she sets a nicely browned apple pie on the table. "They might not be the same as back home, but we like them."

"And we have ice cream too," announces Lydia as she produces a round carton and a scoop.

"I'm impressed," I admit. "Here we are in the middle of nowhere, and you are making us feel totally at home."

We limit the conversation to small talk after this. I have a feeling something is going on between Lydia and her parents, something I can't quite figure out. I know it's ridiculous, but I'm thinking about the whole bride-price thing in this country. Surely her parents aren't trying to keep her here so they can marry her off for profit. No, that's too ridiculous. Still...

TWELVE

I'm surprised at how cool it gets in the evening here. I actually need to put on a sweatshirt to stay warm while we watch an old video. It's called *Groundhog Day*, and I've never seen it before, but it's really pretty funny.

"Well, it's been a long day," says Mrs. Johnson about halfway through the movie. "I think I'll call it a night."

"Me too," says Mr. Johnson. He winks at Lydia. "I think I remember how this one ends."

Lydia laughs. "We've only watched it about a dozen times."

"If anyone wants a hot shower tonight, I'm afraid you'll have to use the bucket," calls Mrs. Johnson. "Lydia can show you how it works."

We thank them and say good night. Finally Bill Murray (in the movie) pulls his act together, and the video ends.

"I'm exhausted," says Sid. "I'm heading for bed too."

"Does anyone want a shower?" asks Lydia. "It can be busy in there in the morning."

"I don't mind taking a shower before bed," I say, imagining how it will be with five adults trying to share one shower tomorrow. "Is it hard to figure out the bucket thing?"

"It's fairly simple," she says, leading me over to the wood cook-stove, where Mrs. Johnson prepared our all-American meal. "This is a hot-water heater." She points to one side of the stove. "See this spigot? The hot water comes from here."

"Oh."

"So you get the bucket from the shower, bring it in here, and fill it about half to two-thirds full of hot water, depending on how hot you like it."

"Right."

"Then you fill it up the rest of the way with cool water from the shower. Here, I'll show you." So we retrieve the bucket from the bathroom. Then she pours in hot water, and we take it back and finish filling it. "Does that temperature feel about right?"

I dip my finger in and nod.

"Then we hang it back up here," she says as she hoists it onto a hook. "When you're ready, you turn the shower nozzle to the left to release the water. And then back to the right to stop it from flowing. Okay?"

"Sounds simple enough."

She points to a closet. "Towels are in there."

"Thanks."

She smiles. "Just remember there's only one gallon of water there. You have to be quick."

I nod. "Okay. This should be fun."

"Good night."

I tell her good night, then hurry to my room to get my pajamas and go back to the bathroom, where I quickly undress, worried that the water will cool off before I even get into the shower. Then I turn the nozzle like she explained, and out comes some very warm water, which actually feels great. I soap up and am totally enjoying the comforting warmth, since it did get fairly cool this evening. Other than the sunshine during the day and the cookstove at night, the Johnsons' home has no source of heat. Then suddenly—just like that—no more water. I tap the bucket and give it a shake to discover that it's empty. Who knew a gallon of water could disappear so quickly? The problem is I'm still soapy. And I'm getting cold.

I consider going back to the kitchen for another bucket of hot water, but what if someone sees me? How embarrassing. Finally I decide to try out the regular shower. Maybe there's enough solar-heated water to finish this off. Naturally, the water coming out of the tap is very cool, but I quickly rinse the soap off and get out to towel dry. I am colder than ever as I put on my summer-weight pajamas and hurry to the bedroom. I layer on my sweatshirt, then climb onto the top bunk. Who knew you could get cold like this in Papua New Guinea?

Now my problem is that I'm wide awake. Taking a cold shower at night isn't exactly relaxing. And as I lie here, still shivering, I can hear what sounds like drumming. At first I think it's simply my overactive imagination, but then I strain to listen and realize, no, it's really drums. It sounds like tribal drums. Occasionally I hear shouts, or maybe it's chanting. I wonder if anyone else in the house is aware of this and whether it's a normal occurrence or something we should be concerned about.

Okay, I know it's crazy, but as I lay there in the dark, I envision tribesmen who are painted up and dancing around the fire, maybe the same guys who tried to rob us on the road earlier today, and I imagine they are planning to come here and get us. Sure, there are bars on the windows, but the rest of this house doesn't seem all that secure. I mean, it's only wood and bamboo. And now, instead of simply being wide awake and cold, I am wide awake, scared, and cold.

"Sid?" I whisper urgently. But she doesn't answer, and I can hear the even sound of breathing that tells me she's probably asleep. I'm sure everyone's asleep. I should be asleep. But what if this is not just my imagination? What if we really are in some kind of danger? I've heard and read such strange stories about New Guinea lately. How can anyone be certain of their safety in a place like this? What am I doing here?

Then I remember what Lydia told me, how she has learned to trust God for her safety. And so, in an attempt to follow her brave example, I begin to pray. I ask God to keep us safe and to help me not to be so frightened. I also ask him to bless our day tomorrow. And finally, I ask him to help us help Lydia. If she really wants to go to med school, I pray that God will show us a way to get her there—and a way to help her parents adjust to this possibility.

I wake up to more strange sounds. Only now it's daylight, and the sounds seem to be from animals. I think perhaps birds.

"It's about time you woke up," says Sid, who is already dressed. "Breakfast is almost ready."

"Sorry," I mumble as I crawl out of bed. "What time is it anyway?"

"It's only seven, but Mr. Johnson wants to get an early start to Mount Hagen."

"I had a hard time getting to sleep last night," I tell her, explaining about the cold shower and the drumming.

"Poor Maddie." She chuckles as she leaves the room.

I hurry to get ready, then go out to see an enticing breakfast spread on the big table and everyone just sitting down. "Sorry I'm late," I say, slipping into a chair.

"Sid told us about your cold shower last night," says Mrs. Johnson. "I'm so sorry."

"I didn't realize how quickly one bucket of water can go," I admit. "I'm sure that won't happen again."

"And then the drumming kept you awake?" asks Mr. Johnson.

"Yes," I say, grateful that he seems to know what I'm talking about. "Is that normal?"

He laughs. "For this time of year it is. The village fellows were practicing for the competition today. They left for Mount Hagen about an hour before daybreak."

"Oh." I nod, feeling even sillier now. "So that's what it was."

Then Mr. Johnson bows his head and blesses the food, and we all dig in.

"Is everyone going to the sing-sing?" asks Sid.

"Not me," says Mrs. Johnson. "I've seen enough sing-sings to last a lifetime."

"I always go," admits Mr. Johnson with a twinkle in his eye. "You just never know what'll happen there."

"That's for sure," says his wife. "Tell them about last year."

So he launches into a story about how there was an actual battle. "It didn't start until after dark," he says. "Usually we don't stay that long, but we had friends from the States who were staying at the hotel there, and they invited us to join them for dinner. Anyway, we were just getting ready to leave when we heard lots of yelling outside. We went to see what was going on. I asked a man on the sidelines, and he said it had started with some young boys just sort of play fighting, you know, and then some women had gotten into it, using real weapons like knives and razors. Finally the men got involved, and they brought out real guns."

"Oh my," says Sid. "Was anyone hurt?"

"Yes." He nods. "Unfortunately, three people were killed, and many others were injured."

"That's just one more reason I don't plan to go this year," says Mrs. Johnson as she passes a plate of pancakes my way.

"It's not always that bad," says Mr. Johnson, "especially since they've changed how the prizes are awarded."

"How's that?" asks Sid as she pours syrup.

"Well, a few years back they would give cash prizes to the teams who took first, second, and third place, and so on."

"Yes," says Mrs. Johnson. "But imagine how angry a team might be if they thought they deserved first prize. Fights often erupted following the competition. It could get very ugly. Soon the tourists were afraid to come."

"So they revamped things," continues Mr. Johnson. "Now, as usual, the prize money is collected from the spectators, but it's equally distributed among all the contestants. Everyone is a winner." He smiles. "Consequently, lots less fighting."

"But even so, you never know." Mrs. Johnson looks at us. "Things can happen. You girls must be especially careful. Stay together. And, Lydia, if you insist on going today, make sure you stay with your father at all times. Do not become separated from the group."

"Yes, Mom, you've already given me this lecture several times."

"I know." She makes what seems a forced smile. "I just want you to be safe. All of you."

"There are several ways to see the show," explains Mr. Johnson. "You can stay on the sidelines and see quite a bit. Or, if you want the full experience, you can buy the pricey tickets and go down and walk around with the dancers."

"Really?" Sid looks surprised. "You can go right down among them?"

"Yes. It's really quite an experience."

"And it's safe?" asks Sid.

"Yes," says Mr. Johnson. "It's during the day, and everyone is mostly focused on performing. And they like having their pictures taken."

"Not like in the old days," says Mrs. Johnson. "We used to hear stories about how nationals would get angry if you took their photo. They thought you were trying to steal their spirits."

"Times have changed." Mr. Johnson sighs.

"I think it'd be fun to go down with the dancers," I say. "Is it very expensive?"

"It's about thirty U.S. dollars per person," he says. "A little steep for our budget."

"How about if we treat?" suggests Sid. "I mean, if that's okay with everyone. I'm sure it would make both Maddie and me feel safer if we could all stay together."

"It's fine with me," says Mr. Johnson. "Although I'm sure you two would be perfectly safe if you just stayed together."

"Well, I'd feel better if you and Lydia joined us."

So it seems to be settled. We'll all be down amid the dancers today, getting the full experience. I'm really looking forward to it. Mrs. Johnson has prepared a picnic lunch, and the plan is to be home in time for a late dinner. Once again she warns us to be careful as we tell her good-bye.

"Don't worry, Mom," says Lydia. "God is watching over us."

Mrs. Johnson frowns slightly, then nods. "Yes, I know." She waves from the porch, and we pile back into the Land Rover.

"How do the other people from the village get there?" I ask.

"There's a shared village truck," he explains. "The competitors took that over early this morning. Some have already walked there. Some will go by bus. We'll probably see a fair number of walkers on the road today, hoping to catch a ride."

He's right. The closer we get to Mount Hagen, the more we see people walking. Some are wearing costumes, which are amazingly bright and colorful. Some just have on regular clothes. Most of the women carry large string bags, almost like fishnet. The straps on the bags are worn over the tops of their heads, and the bags, which look full and heavy, hang down to the middle of their backs.

"What do the women carry in those bags?" I ask.

"Those are *bilums*," says Lydia from where she's sitting in front with her dad. "They carry all sorts of things. Food, clothes, even babies."

"Babies?"

"Yes, they pad them with clothes and things, then nestle them in. I imagine it's a fairly comfortable ride."

"But they must get heavy," I say.

"New Guinean women are strong," says Mr. Johnson in a slightly sad tone. "They're very hard workers and are used to carrying a load."

"Does that mean the men don't work so hard?" I ask.

Lydia laughs and rolls her eyes.

"Well, I'm sure the men *think* they work hard enough," says her dad, "but the truth is, it's the women who do most of the work. They work in the gardens, planting and harvesting; they take care of the children, fix all the meals. Basically they take care of the family."

"What do the men do?"

"Oh, they hunt sometimes. And they build the houses, although the women help with that too. And some men will go out and get jobs to support their family. Sometimes you'll have a very industrious man who supports a number of families back in the village. But that's not the norm."

"What sort of jobs do they get?"

"There's not a lot for the untrained worker up here in the highlands. Of course, there's always mining. That's pretty hard work, although the pay is relatively good. The problem is that many of our people aren't used to having that much money, and a lot of the men tend to waste it. There's a growing alcohol problem here. That's really taken a toll on families in the highlands."

"And the lowlands too," adds Lydia.

"That's too bad."

"So what would you say is the main industry in New Guinea?" asks Sid. "What brings in the most income for the nationals? Is it mining? coffee plantations? tea?"

"To be honest, it's probably crime," says Mr. Johnson sadly.

"Seriously?"

"You'd be amazed at how many villages are supported by criminal activity," says Mr. Johnson. "And many people think it's completely acceptable—well, as long as they're not the victims. The criminals are called *rascals,* and they are everywhere."

"What about the police?" asks Sid. "Do they try to crack down on them?"

"Unfortunately, the police can be part of the problem. Many are as morally corrupt as the rascals."

"Many are even worse," says Lydia in a solemn voice.

"Yes." Her dad nods sadly. "It's true."

"So it really is a widespread problem then?" Sid asks.

"Very much so." He sighs. "I suppose that makes the rascals feel even more validated for their lives of crime. Some probably consider themselves to be a Robin Hood."

"Stealing from the rich to feed the poor?" I say.

"Yes. It's justifiable to them."

"And some feel the need to protect themselves from the police," Lydia points out. "They have their own tribal gang of rascals, are fully armed, and think nothing of engaging with any form of police or security that invades their territory."

"And what do the police do?" asks Sid.

"Look away, keep a safe distance." Mr. Johnson just shakes his head.

"So what sorts of crimes do they make the most profit from?" asks Sid.

"Well, you had your own close brush with carjacking. They steal a car and sell it to a village. That's just one way rascals capitalize on crime. Trust me, there are many more. By the way, has anyone warned you about passport thefts?"

"The USAID woman in Australia told us to be careful," says Sid. "She suggested we keep them on our person at all times, in our money belts."

Lydia laughs. "That's the first place the rascals look."

"Really?"

"Unfortunately," says Mr. Johnson, "we hear more cases of tourists being robbed than almost anything. The rascals assume the tourists are wealthy, and by New Guinean standards, they are. Plus, they're usually carrying money, credit cards, and passports. Their desire for money is obvious, but they also know how to use the plastic. And lately they've even come up with a clever use for passports."

"What's that?"

"After they steal them—and they do usually look in the money belt first—they sell the documents to someone who has a connection with a passport seller in Port Moresby."

"So the passports are eventually resold?"

"Yes, usually to the original owner."

"What?"

Lydia laughs. "Yes. So, if by chance your passports are stolen, which we hope isn't the case, all you need to do is find out who's selling passports in Port Moresby that week, contact them, and see if they have yours."

"They usually go for anywhere between fifty and five hundred kina, depending on how desperate or determined the customer might be. If you're firm with them and don't get them angry at you, you might get off for less."

"That is so bizarre," I say.

"Why wouldn't the tourist who's been robbed simply call the police if they discover someone with their passport?" asks Sid. "Why don't they tell the police to get it back for them so they don't have to pay for it?"

"By the time the police got there, if they even came, the passport seller would be long gone, and you'd probably never see your passport again. Most tourists figure out, sooner or later, that it's not worth it."

"Talk about your Catch-22."

"Yep." His expression is grim. "Things have sure changed a lot during the time we've been in New Guinea."

"How long is that?" asks my aunt.

"Brenda and I first came over just a few months before Independence, back in 1975."

"So you were here for Independence?" I say. I've read a little about how this country declared itself independent several decades ago. "What was that like?"

"Surprisingly, it went off quietly. There were some small snags but nothing like what the Australians expected as they were making their big getaway. Of course, their gloomy predictions played out later. At the time, everything was totally new to us. Brenda and I came here straight out of jungle camp. We really didn't know what to expect. And we were ready for anything."

"Jungle camp?"

He laughs. "Yes, I know that sounds strange. But it's the last stage of training for translators. Sort of like boot camp, to see whether or not you can survive out in the bush. We'd already gone through SIL school together in Dallas. That was where we met, actually. We'd both just graduated from college, and God had called us both to translation work. We got married shortly after the first year of translation school."

"So you've been translating for more than thirty years?" I say in astonishment. "Wow, that's real commitment."

"Well, when God calls you to do something, what can you say?"

"And you've been with the Lomokako people the whole time?" asks Sid.

"No. We actually started out in a village that another couple had been working in. They had to leave because of the wife's health problems. That village was on the Sepik River."

"Where's that?" I ask.

"Not too far from here as the crow flies. It's on the north side of the island, opposite of Port Moresby. If you have time, it's an area well worth seeing. Anyway, Brenda and I started out there. We didn't have kids yet, and we were ripe for an adventure. But we quickly discovered it wasn't easy to pick up where someone else had left off. And the villagers didn't fully trust us, especially at first. They liked the other translators, and I think they blamed us for their leaving. Anyway, we finished up the New Testament in about nine years and asked to be transferred to the highlands for a new assignment."

"Do you like the highlands better?" I ask, thinking that if I lived in this country, this is where I'd want to be.

"Yes. We really felt called to this part of the country. In some ways it's more rugged and less civilized, but we like it."

"So how long have you been in this village?"

"We came here in 1986. The boys were about two and four. Young enough that they think of this as their first home." He turns and looks at Lydia. "And we got here just in time to get our daughter."

The car slows down, and I look up to see a throng of people walking down the middle of the road, blocking our way. Mr. Johnson rolls down his window and calls out in a friendly tone. They turn and look at him curiously, and he calls out something else.

Okay, I'm getting worried now. I've heard about roadblocks, and this certainly looks like one. There are at least twenty of them, mostly men, and I'm thinking that if they wanted, they could easily overtake this vehicle. But then they simply smile and wave, calling back to Mr. Johnson, and it's obvious that this is just a friendly encounter. They slowly break apart and allow us to pass by, slapping the sides of the vehicle as we go. Mr. Johnson calls out what sounds like *thank you* in pidgin and some kind of greeting.

I take in a deep breath, glancing at Sid to see if she was as worried as I was just now. She gives me a little smile, but I can tell it was a bit unsettling to her too. For some reason that actually makes no sense, I feel better.

THIRTEEN

*I*t's almost eleven when we arrive in Mount Hagen. Mr. Johnson pays one kina to park in a field on the edge of town, then we get out and walk toward the sounds of drums, chanting, and singing. There's energy in the air, and I almost feel like I'm a kid again, like I'm on my way to the circus or the county fair for the first time. People are everywhere. Some in costume hurry over to where the sounds are coming from as if they are late. Others move along more casually. But there are very few white people.

"This is exciting," I say as we walk along a dusty road.

"It is, isn't it?" says Mr. Johnson. "Even after all these years, I still look forward to this event."

"People come halfway around the world to see it," says Lydia.

"I can understand that," says Sid. "From what I've heard, there's nothing else like it anywhere."

Soon we're at the edge of the event. Sid goes forward and purchases four tickets, and then Mr. Johnson leads us down to where the performers are dancing. It's an amazing scene of color and motion and sound. I don't think I can take it all in—painted faces and millions of kinds of feathers and shells and colorful vegetation. Every possible sort of adornment and ornament seems to be here. Most are natural, but there are also things like flattened Coke cans strung together to make a vest, and I notice one man wearing a faux-leopard bra that could've originated at Victoria's Secret. I try not to laugh, but a bra! I wonder if he knows that it's meant for a woman. Most participants, though, are wearing traditional costumes. And I notice that some of the dance teams are made up of women. Mr. Johnson explains that this wasn't always the case and that the men and women never mix. It's always a male team or a female team.

"Those are Asaro mudmen," he says, pointing to the tribesmen who are wearing these oversize masks that appear to be made from mud or clay. Their bodies are coated with pale mud, giving them an almost ghostly appearance, except for the expressions on the masks, which are friendly and almost humorous. "There are Chimbu mudmen too."

The teams take great care to dress alike, so there's no mixing up who is with whom. I notice one dance team painted in black and white to resemble skeletons, and at first it's slightly scary. But Mr. Johnson explains about the tribe they're from and how this is their tradition. It's amazing to be able to walk right up to these people, so strangely dressed, and simply snap their photos. Some even smile, often exposing stained or missing teeth. Others give us their fiercest looks, which I find a little creepy. Then after the picture is taken, they often smile, and I can hardly believe I'm looking at the same person.

All in all, I think these people are just friendly, fun loving, and looking for a good time. More than ever I really like this country. I can understand how Papua New Guinea could grow on a person. Quite honestly, I've never seen brighter, more open smiles than the ones I've witnessed on nationals today. They seem genuine to me.

Some of the performers recognize Mr. Johnson, and after a quick "remember me" introduction, he recognizes them. Some grew up in his village but live in a city now. Some have gone on to school. And amid these rustic and tribal people, I discover there are doctors, lawyers, and other professionals. "It's a celebration of their culture," Mr. Johnson tells us after we're introduced to a dentist from Goroka, whose teeth are in great condition. "They're proud of their tribal roots."

"They should be," says Sid. "It's a rich heritage. Not many people in this generation can claim anything even slightly like this."

Finally we're all getting hungry, and we head back to the Land Rover to have a break and a late lunch. Lydia pulls out a large blanket to spread on the trampled grass, and we all sit down to eat. It's after two now, and the plan is to return for another hour or so before we head back to the village, hopefully before dark.

"I can't believe I've used up almost all of the space on my digital camera," says Sid as she views some of the shots she's just taken.

"And I'm out of film too," I say. "I think I took three rolls already."

"Well, maybe you can put the cameras aside now," suggests Mr. Johnson. "When we go back, you can just be free to look around, to watch and enjoy the people without the distraction of taking photos."

"Good idea," says Sid.

Lydia stretches out along the side of the blanket now, closing her eyes.

"Are you tired, Lydia?" asks her dad in a kind but concerned voice. "Do you want a nap?"

"No, I'm fine."

"That sounds like a good idea to me," I say, stretching out in the sun next to Lydia. "Ah, this feels good."

So we all lie down for a few minutes. It's weird feeling the prickly grass through my thin cotton shirt, hearing the constant background sounds of drumming and chanting, and smelling a mixture of wood smoke and vegetation in the air. Although I know I'm in a totally foreign place right now, there's something about the earthiness here that feels familiar. Maybe it's like our farm. Or maybe it's something more. I'm sure I could never explain it. But it's sort of cool. And it's good to feel this relaxed, like I'm not worried about anything right now, like I know that God really is watching over us and that we're safe in his hands. I take a long deep breath, hold it, and then exhale slowly.

"Well," says Mr. Johnson, standing up and stretching his arms to the sky, "before we all nod off, I suggest we trek back over to the celebration and get in the last of our afternoon." So we all pull ourselves back to our feet, pack up the picnic things, and head back toward the music.

There we roam around together, watching various miniperformances and clapping and cheering the teams on. Eventually we come across the locals from the Lomokako village, where the Johnsons live, and I'm surprised to see that Peter is among the performers today. He grins at us and shakes his spear, then introduces us to his buddies. After that, they do a short routine, which is really good. I wish I had a video camera so I could take this home to share with my family. Peter's face is painted red and yellow, and Lydia explains that his amazing headdress—a combination of feathers from birds of paradise (the national bird), lorikeets, and parrots—is a family heirloom that he will one day pass down to his son. It fans out about two feet all around his head and is really spectacular.

"I've never seen so many different kinds of feathers," I tell her. "Are they all from New Guinea?"

She nods. "We have more than six hundred different species of birds here."

"Wow, that's amazing. I mean, considering the size of the country."

"Yes, we're an amazing little country." She gives me a funny smile. "In oh so many ways."

It seems we've all lost track of the time, but finally Mr. Johnson tells us that we need to get on the road. "Soon the drinking will begin," he says in a slightly urgent voice as we begin to wind our way back through the even more boisterous crowd.

Lydia points at a performer staggering between his two buddies, his headdress sitting cockeyed on his head. "Looks like it's already begun for some of them," she says.

Her dad nods. "We don't want to be here when it starts getting out of hand."

It's close to five o'clock by the time we're back in the Land Rover and heading out of town. I seriously doubt we can make it back to the village before dark. I wonder if this is a problem. But as we drive the curving mountain road, it seems surprisingly clear of pedestrian traffic. In fact, there is hardly any traffic at all. Hopefully this means everyone is still partying in Mount Hagen.

Even so, I can't help but remember what Mr. Johnson said about the crime rate. I pat my money belt, worried that one of those rascals might've taken it somehow as we were being jostled by the crowd.

"Still there?" asks Sid, looking worried as she pats down her mid-section too.

I laugh. "Yes, but I was thinking about the warnings about passports and money belts getting stolen."

"Anything missing?" asks Mr. Johnson.

"We seem to be intact," says Sid. "But it does make me curious. How would you recommend we carry these things?"

"Well, if you're staying in a reliable hotel, you might want to put them in the hotel safe."

"What about when we're in transit?" she asks.

"I think you're smart to carry a purse," says Lydia. "But only with a bit of spending money in it. Sort of like a decoy. And use a money belt that's thin enough not to be noticed beneath your clothes. If you're in an area where you feel you really could be at risk, I'd put a credit card in my bra."

Mr. Johnson laughs now. "Of course, some rascals have been known to take the clothes right off a person's back."

"You're kidding," I say.

"I wish I were."

"Whoa." I try to imagine how horrible it would feel to be robbed and stripped naked. Of course, this makes me realize there are even worse things that could happen to a person.

"Okay," says Lydia. "Enough of scaring our guests half to death. You are perfectly safe with us."

"You don't think we'll encounter any rascals on the road?" I say in a tentative tone.

"I doubt it," says Mr. Johnson. "I think they're all celebrating in

Mount Hagen. The festival continues into tomorrow. It's too early for them to leave now."

"And after it ends?" asks Sid.

"Well, then I'd be a little more careful," he admits. "And I probably wouldn't be out driving after dark either."

Fortunately, we make it back to the village without a hitch. And I am truly relieved to get out of the vehicle and go back into the Johnsons' house. I'm so amazed by how much I feel at home with these people. More than ever I'm hoping there's a way we can help Lydia to finish her college education. But I don't want to bring it up again. Not after her parents' reaction last night. Maybe Sid will have some ideas.

After another good, all-American meal of hamburgers and potato salad, Mr. Johnson sits us down for a pidgin lesson. "You can't go traipsing around the country barely able to speak," he says as he hands us a printed sheet of paper. "This is what I call a traveler's cheat sheet. Sort of like pidgin crib notes."

I glance down at the paper to see that it has commonly used phrases in pidgin and English, along with their phonetic spelling. Very helpful. And the more we work on it, the simpler it all seems. I think anyone could learn to speak pidgin. Since I already speak fairly good Spanish, maybe I'll be able to say that I'm trilingual by the time I leave New Guinea. Of course, I doubt there's much use for pidgin outside of this country. Still, it's fun to learn.

Travelers' Cheat Sheet

Apinun [ap-ee-noon]
  Good afternoon.

balus [ball-oos] aircraft

bilas [bee-laws]
  decoration or uniform

Em hamas? [em how-mus]
  How much is that?

Gut nait [goot nite] Good night.

haus sik [house seek] hospital

Helpim mi plis [halp-eem me plees]
  Help me please.

Inap mi kisim poto?
  [ee-nop me kees-eem poe-toe]
  May I take a photo?

ka—car

kago [caw-go] luggage

kaikai—food

klostu [close-too] near or close by

lapun [lah-poon]
  old man or woman

longwe tumas [long-way too-maws]
  a very long way or too far

man—man or male

mani [maw-nee] money

manki [man-kee]
  older children and teenagers

meri [merry] woman or female

Mi laik baim [me-like-buy-em]
  I would like to buy.

Mi no klia gut [me no klee-ah goot]
  I do not understand.

Mi no laikim [me no like-em]
  I do not like it.

Mi no save [me no saw-vay]
  I don't know.

Mi stap gut [me stop goot]
  I am fine.

Moning [mow-neeng] Good morning.

Nogat [no gat] No

pikinini [peek-ee-nee-nee]
  baby or very young child

ples balus [place ball-oos] airport

Ples bilong yu we?
  [place bee-long you way]
  Where are you from?

Soim mi [sew-eem me] Show me.

Tenkyu [tank you] Thank you.

Toilet we? [toilet way]
  Where is the toilet?

Tok isi [toke eesee] Speak slowly.

Wanem nem bilong yu?
  [wa-name name bee-long you]
  What is your name?

wantok [wan-toke]
  countryman or friend

wara [wa-rah] water

yangpela [yawng-pay-la]
  young man or woman

Yumi go we? [you-me go way]
  Where are we going?

Yu stap gut? [you stop goot]
  How are you?

FOURTEEN

I manage to take a proper bucket shower Saturday night, carefully rationing the water so that I can (1) turn on the spigot showerhead and quickly soak my hair and body, (2) turn off the spigot showerhead while I thoroughly soap my body and then quickly shampoo my hair, (3) then thoroughly rinse, allowing the very warm water to take the chill off. Okay, this means I don't shampoo my hair twice, like I would at home, but I'm going for the natural look here anyway. I've been letting my curls pretty much go wild, thinking I almost fit in with the locals this way. If I get too hot, I just pull my tangled mop back and secure it on top of my head with a barrette. Not terribly glamorous, but it works. I use Lydia's hair dryer but am concerned about pulling too much electricity from the generator and stop after a few minutes.

Everyone seems worn out after a rather long day, and we all turn in early this evening. Before we go to bed, the Johnsons tell us that they usually sleep a little later on Sundays.

"Our day of rest," says Mr. Johnson.

"Church service is around ten," says his wife. "Before that, we usually just have a quick, light breakfast."

"Sounds great," says Sid. "I'd love to sleep in a little."

And tonight when I go to bed, I'm warm and tired and not the least bit worried about the tribal uprising I imagined last night. How ridiculous.

But I wake up abruptly in the morning. It feels as if the bed is moving, and I'm worried that maybe I weigh too much and I'm going to collapse onto my poor aunt. So I leap out of bed, and to my amazement the bamboo floor is moving too, sort of rocking and rolling, almost like on a ship.

"What's going on?" I yell, waking my aunt, who somehow has managed to peacefully sleep through this horrifying experience.

"What?" she says sleepily. "What's wrong?"

"The house!" I gasp, still feeling a slight tremor beneath my feet. "It's moving. Can't you feel it?"

"Huh?" She sort of blinks.

Then it stops. Just like that. "I woke up, and the bed was moving," I say. "Then I got out, and the floor was moving too. I think the whole house was moving."

She sighs. "You must've had a dream, Maddie."

"It was real," I protest. "I felt it."

"It's not even seven," she says groggily. "Go back to bed, silly girl."

There's no way I can go back to sleep now. I know the house was moving. I felt it. Something seems very wrong here, and I plan on finding out what it is. I quickly dress and go out into the quiet house. But no one is up, and everything looks just as it did when we went to bed last night. I pace a bit, tiptoeing about as I peek out the louvered glass windows to see if anyone is out and about yet.

I notice that the sky looks cloudy today, the kind of foreboding clouds that are dark and heavy and seem to loom close to the ground. The village is peaceful, and other than some stray pigs, which Lydia told me are pretty much left to come and go as they please, no one is stirring. I hear a rooster crow and wonder if that means it's time for people to start getting up. But everything remains still and sleepy. Besides the ticking of the clock, it's very quiet here. I begin to think that Sid was right. I must've dreamed the whole thing.

"You're up early," says Lydia as she emerges from her room wearing a plaid flannel bathrobe.

"My bed was shaking," I tell her. "And I got up, and the floor was shaking too. Sid didn't even feel it, but I know it was for real."

She sort of laughs, then nods. "Yes, it was for real. It was an earthquake."

"An *earthquake*?" My eyes widen. "Seriously? We just had an earthquake?"

She nods as she sits on the couch, pulling her legs up under her.

"Are we in any danger?"

"I don't think so."

"Aren't you even a little bit scared?"

"No. We have them all the time."

"All the time?" How is she not horrified by this?

"Well, not *all* the time. But we have a lot of them. My brothers and I used to feel like earthquakes were scheduled for Saturday mornings, because for a while it seemed they *only* happened on Saturday mornings. Naturally, it was a day we wanted to sleep in, so I guess we noticed it more. Maybe earthquakes have switched to Sundays now."

"That's so weird," I say. "I've never felt an earthquake before."

"Don't you have them in the Pacific Northwest?" she asks. "I thought I'd heard you have active volcanoes up there."

"Well, we do have some active volcanoes. Mount St. Helens blew its top twenty-some-odd years ago, before I was born. And the mountain still rumbles, and scientists are always watching. But I've never actually felt an earthquake before." I smile. "Hey, that's pretty cool. I can go home and tell people that I survived an earthquake in Papua New Guinea."

"We actually had a really bad earthquake here in 1998," she says, "on the north coast. It was followed by a horrible tsunami."

"Really?"

"Yes. Thousands died, and thousands more were left homeless."

"I don't remember even hearing about it."

"News about Papua New Guinea doesn't usually make the headlines around the globe. And, of course, our little tsunami wasn't anything compared to the one in the Indian Ocean in 2004. That was incredibly devastating."

"Still, with thousands of people being killed, you'd think that would make the news in a big way."

Lydia shrugs. "Maybe it did. Maybe you just didn't notice. I mean, you were still a kid in 1998. I remember I was about thirteen, and it was the first year I lived in a children's home and went to school on base. Everyone there was so upset when it happened. I was really scared too. I actually thought it was going to be the end of the world for everyone." She sort of laughs. "Anyway, they let us go home to stay with our parents for a while and be reassured that it wasn't really the end of life as we knew it. Then it was back to business as usual."

"Was it hard living away from home when you were so young?" I ask her. Okay, I can only imagine how I would've felt under those same circumstances. Good grief, I haven't even left home to go to school yet, and I'm twenty! It's kind of embarrassing.

She nods. "Yes, it was hard at first. But I had my brothers. We were in the same children's home. Having them there was almost like being at home. Of course, they were teenagers by then and already had their friends and activities. But it helped knowing they were there. Especially if anyone gave me a problem."

"Who would give you a problem?"

"Oh, you know how kids can be. Oddly enough, I became the minority at school on base. Almost all the other kids were white."

"Wow, that must've been weird."

"It was. But it helped me to understand how my family feels out here in the village where they're the minority."

"Yeah," I admit. "I've felt sort of like that myself, just being in New Guinea. The pale faces kind of stick out."

"The funny thing was, I think I'd started to forget that I was New Guinean. Not that I thought I was white exactly, but I knew I was different from the rest of the kids in our village. I suppose I thought of myself as American, you know, since my family was American. But when I got to Ukarumpa, some of the kids at school made sure I knew I was different from them too. I guess I wasn't sure exactly where I fit in."

"That seems odd," I say. "I mean, since the kids had come here with their families to be missionaries to New Guinean people. I'd think they'd be more loving and kind and open-minded."

She laughs quietly. "Keep in mind that it's the parents who came here to be missionaries. The kids just get dragged along for the ride. Or, like my brothers, they're born here. Either way, it's not really their choice."

"So do you think kids resent having missionary parents?"

"No, I don't think so. Not for the most part anyway. But you always have a few who act out. Just like anywhere else. And I suppose it didn't help matters that I was a fairly competitive kid. More than ever, I wanted to prove myself, and I guess I was sort of a show-off sometimes."

"I can't imagine you being a show-off," I admit. "You seem like such a mature and well-grounded person to me."

She smiles. "Thanks. I hope I've grown up a little over the years. Back then, I felt the need to show the others that I was as good as they were, that I could keep up. And as I got older, it got worse. I felt like I had to be better than my peers. I had to get the best grades, be the best at soccer or whatever activity I was interested in at the time. And, naturally, that made some kids—especially a certain couple of girls whose parents lived on base—target me."

"I've known girls like that too."

She smiles. "See, there really isn't anything new under the sun, is there?"

"Did you have some good friends too?" I ask, suddenly worried that poor, sweet Lydia might've been shunned by everyone.

"Oh yes, of course. I had some wonderful friends who I'm still very close to. We stay in touch through e-mail, and we hope to have a reunion in a few years. I miss them."

"I thought I heard voices," says Mr. Johnson as he enters the room. "What got you girls up so early this morning?"

"The earthquake woke Maddie." Lydia rises from her spot on the sofa and goes into the kitchen.

He chuckles. "I guess we forgot to warn you about earthquakes. We get them occasionally. Nothing to be overly concerned about. Well, unless the house starts to cave in. In that case, make a fast break for the wide open spaces outside."

"Gee, thanks."

He wads up some paper and places kindling in the cookstove. "The worst time for earthquakes, at least up here in the highlands, is during the rainy season."

"Why's that?" I ask.

"Mud slides." He lights the match and steps back. "They can be lethal. Whole villages have been buried. Not a single survivor."

I shudder. "That's horrible."

He nods. "So just be glad you're here during the dry season."

"Does that mean it doesn't rain?" I ask, glancing outside at the thick gray clouds.

He laughs. "No. It always rains. It just rains less. Sometimes we'll have several days without rain. In fact, it's been pretty dry lately."

"I'll make the coffee," says Lydia, filling the pot from the sink.

"And it does look like we're in for some rain today," he observes. "Too bad for the sing-sing festivities. But the locals are used to it. Hopefully, it won't make the road too bad for the travelers. It's not unusual to have a wreck or two when the sing-sing ends anyway. Just another reason we were smart to go on the first day of the celebration.

Pity the poor tourist who has a wreck and doesn't have the wits to get out of there before payback time."

"There sure are a lot of things to be concerned with around here," I say as Mr. Johnson puts some bigger pieces of wood on the fire. "Earthquakes, mud slides, paybacks, crime, diseases—"

"And we haven't told you about the snakes yet."

"Snakes?" I feel a shiver down my spine.

"Oh, Dad," scolds Lydia. "Give her a break. The poor girl just survived an earthquake, for Pete's sake."

This makes him laugh, and for the moment I'm spared hearing about the snakes. Great!

Soon everyone is up, and I make Mr. Johnson inform my aunt that we really did experience an earthquake this morning.

"I thought she was just dreaming," says Sid as she sips her coffee. "I didn't feel a thing."

"The top bunk usually feels it the most," says Mrs. Johnson. "I think it must sway more up there."

"Yes," agrees Lydia. "That was Caleb's bed, and he was always complaining about feeling earthquakes that the rest of us missed."

"Of course, Jeremy used to worry that the top bunk was going to collapse and fall on him someday," adds Mr. Johnson as he sets a plate of fresh fruit on the table. "Especially as Caleb got bigger."

"I had that exact same thought myself," I admit. "I was afraid I was going to crush my aunt." I nod to her. "One of the reasons I jumped out of bed. You should thank me, Sid."

She smiles. "Thank you very much."

After breakfast is finished and cleaned up, we head over to the village church, which is just off to the far side of the little round houses. It's starting to rain as we enter the long, rectangular structure that is their church. The floor is made of cement, and a palm-thatched roof is supported by rough columns of wood, but there are no walls, no windows, no doors. The structure is completely open. About thirty people are already seated, filling the rows of rough-hewn benches— the men and boys on one side, women and small children on the other. I suspect that this separation of the sexes must be a cultural thing, but I make a mental note to ask Lydia about it later.

"Air conditioned," I whisper to her as we sit on one of the back benches.

Lydia smiles. "Yes. God's air conditioning."

More people trickle in, taking their spots on the benches, and finally a man steps up to the front and begins to tune a slightly beat-up guitar. Then he starts to lead us in singing. I'm impressed with the enthusiasm of the congregation as they join in, but it quickly becomes clear that they don't know how to stay on key very well. In fact, it sounds more like chanting than singing. And when he plays a song I actually recognize, I'm even more aware of how different their musical style is from what I'm used to. And yet it's so amazing, so authentic, so heartfelt, I think.

For a long while, I just stand there, letting it all soak in: the rain, which is pouring down from the sloped roof; the low, nasal, yet rhythmic sound of the chanted hymns and songs; the open-air church; the slightly out-of-tune guitar. Then it hits me. I am in the highlands of Papua New Guinea, worshiping God with sincere believers. And I can't think of any word to describe how I feel right now besides *awestruck.* I am in awe of God and in awe of these people he created. It blows my mind.

I know with certainty that their singing/chanting is a thing of immense beauty to God. In some ways I think this sort of worship must be even more beautiful than the fanciest church with the biggest pipe organ and the most talented choir. At least it is to me, and I suspect God agrees. Not that God makes comparisons like we humans tend to do, but if he did…

After quite a long stint of singing/chanting, another man goes to the front to speak. Lydia whispers to me that he'll be preaching in tok ples. Consequently, Sid and I are the only ones here who don't understand. But the young man preaches with such passion and enthusiasm that I almost feel like I know what he's saying. Anyway, whatever it is, he seems genuine, and the people listening seem eager to hear, nodding and even murmuring at times. It's all pretty impressive. And it gives me great hope for a country I'd originally misjudged.

It's still raining, and I notice the water is pooling up around the perimeter of the church. It's a good thing the floor in here is built up of cement, because it's the only thing remaining dry. But as I notice this, I notice something else too, something that I think is a little weird. I wonder if I'm the only one who sees it. There are frogs hopping around on the cement floor, underneath the benches and around people's bare feet. They're fairly big frogs too, about two to three inches in diameter, I'm guessing. I glance over at Lydia, but her eyes are straight forward, focused on the speaker. I glance over at Sid, who's on the other side of Lydia, but she too seems oblivious. Suddenly I remember the plague of the frogs on Egypt. Hopefully, God isn't trying to send us some kind of message. Then I recall what I've heard about animals sensing a natural disaster like an earthquake or tsunami, and I start to feel more seriously concerned.

Now, unlike my opinion on snakes, it's not that I'm afraid of or even dislike frogs. I am, after all, a farm girl. But all these hopping critters are becoming more and more unsettling. I want to know why they're here. And I'm surprised that not even the children seem to notice them or care. Then I see one particularly large frog just sitting there, looking straight toward the pulpit as if he's listening and taking it all in. It makes me want to laugh. But I control myself since it seems the preacher is at a serious part of his sermon, and I'd hate to spoil it for everyone. But at last, when the final prayer and song are finished, I ask Lydia what's going on here.

"So, are these frogs here to worship or what?" I say.

She laughs. "No, they're just coming in out of the rain."

"I thought frogs liked water."

She nods to where the land surrounding the church is starting to resemble a large muddy pond. "I think they get overwhelmed sometimes."

I have to laugh. "So when frogs get overwhelmed, they come to church? That makes sense."

"Yes. People should follow their example."

And I think Lydia is right. People should follow their example.

FIFTEEN

Later that afternoon Sid asks Mr. and Mrs. Johnson what part of the country they'd recommend we see during the following week.

"Well, if it were me, I'd go to the Sepik," says Mr. Johnson. "It's a fascinating region. And Western Sepik is the best." He pulls out a map and begins to show us how a river winds along the northern part of Papua New Guinea. "It's similar to the Amazon in ways. Very remote. You'll even see crocodiles."

"Crocodiles?" I say with interest.

"Yes. The village we worked in had some incredible crocodile hunters. One time they actually caught a saltwater croc. Somehow it made it inland about a hundred miles. It was sixteen feet long."

"Sixteen feet?" I try to imagine this, and Mr. Johnson actually gets up and shows us about how long that would be.

"Wow," I say. "That sounds pretty exciting."

"I could arrange for you to visit Kauani," he says.

"Is that in Hawaii?" I ask, immediately knowing it's probably not.

"That's our old village in the Sepik," says Mrs. Johnson.

"Our good friends Tom and Donna Hanover are working there now. They picked up right where we left off."

"Really?" says Sid with interest. "Do you think they'd want visitors?"

Mrs. Johnson laughs. "Are you kidding? They'd love visitors. Tom and Donna are some of the most hospitable translators in the country. Their kids are back in the States going to college now, and I know they get lonely at times."

"I'll go see if I can get them on the radio," says Mr. Johnson suddenly. "And I'll check with JAARS too. See if they can get you a flight out there."

"Thanks!" says Sid. "That would be fantastic."

While Sid and the Johnsons are working out the travel details, Lydia points out that the sun is shining. "We could take a walk," she says.

"That sounds great," I agree. "I'd like to get a better look at your village."

"And I know that Peter would love for you to meet his wife and daughter," she says as we head outside. "He's still at the sing-sing. I think he makes a point to stay there to ensure that his male friends don't end up in some sort of trouble." She chuckles.

"His wife didn't go with him?"

Lydia shakes her head. "No, she's pregnant, and I think her due date's not too far off."

So we walk around the village, and Lydia introduces me to so many people that I soon lose track of the names. Some of the villagers are still at the sing-sing, but the older people and young children are here. Everyone is very friendly, and their smiles are so bright and sweet that their whole faces light up.

"I wish I could see inside a house," I tell Lydia. "I'm curious what they're like."

"We'll see what we can do," she says as we go up to a house that's close to the church and seems a little nicer than some of the others. Or maybe it's just newer.

"This is Peter's wife," says Lydia as we approach a smiling woman sitting in the doorway of this house. She has on a faded-print, smock-style dress, and her hands rest on top of her rounded belly. Lydia told me these garments are called *meri* dresses, and they seem to be the most popular fashion among the village women. Designed to accommodate a body's changes through pregnancy and into old age, they look comfortable.

"Mataswai," says Lydia, "this is my friend Maddie. She's a friend of Peter's too."

Mataswai stands up, takes my hand, and gives it a warm squeeze. "I am happy to know you."

"You speak English?"

"*Liklik.*"

I think about this. "Little?"

Lydia nods. "That's right."

A tiny girl suddenly appears from behind Mataswai. "Thees ees my daughter, Hannah," says her mother. "Say hallo, Hannah." But the little girl ducks her head behind her mother.

"Hello, Hannah," I call out.

Then Lydia says something to Mataswai in tok ples. First Mataswai hesitates, and then she puts her hand over her mouth. Then she nods. "Yesa, eet's all right. Come een. Come een." Then she steps back into her house and waves us inside.

It takes my eyes a few seconds to adjust to the dim light. The floor, not unlike the one in the Johnson home, is made of springy bamboo and sits less than a foot off the ground. In the center of the house is a fire pit with softly glowing red embers. It smells smoky in here but not in a bad way. It reminds me of that camping scent, the way your sweatshirt might smell after you've stood in front of a camp-fire for several nights.

There isn't any furniture to speak of in here. Just a very low wooden table near the fire, which I assume Mataswai uses as a kitchen since there are some metal pots and bowls and cooking things there. There are mats and blankets on the floor on the opposite side, and I'm guessing that's used as a sleeping area. The whole house is about twelve feet wide. Very cozy. Once again I'm reminded of camping. It feels sort of like the old canvas tent Dad used to haul out when we went up to the lake for a weekend of fishing. Only we didn't have a campfire inside. That would've been too dangerous.

"How does the smoke get out?" I ask, noticing there isn't a chimney.

Lydia points to a small hole in the center of the roof. "There."

"What about the rain?"

"It's not much of a problem. They're used to it."

"Very nice," I say to Mataswai. "And it's warm in here."

"Warm." She nods, rubbing her hands over the fire. "Yesa. Eet's warm."

Lydia points to something in the fire. "May I show it to Maddie?"

Mataswai nods, and Lydia removes a green bundle and slowly unwraps it until I see what looks like some kind of root that's the color of ashes.

"It's taro," she says. "It's related to a sweet potato. Very starchy and bland."

"Is it good?" I ask Mataswai.

"Yes. Eet's good." Then she motions with her hand, like she wants me to sample some for myself. *"Kaikaim."*

"Go ahead," says Lydia. "It might be your only chance to taste *kaukau.*"

"Kaukau?"

"Pidgin for 'sweet potato.' Go ahead and try it."

"Are you sure?" I look at her, uncertain whether I want to or not. It's one thing to sample Guinness in Ireland, where at least I can be sure it's been bottled hygienically.

"It won't hurt you," promises Lydia.

So I break off a small piece and put it in my mouth and chew. It sort of has the texture of a yam, a very fibrous yam, but the flavor makes me think of what an old sock might taste like. Even so, I swallow it and force a smile and thank Mataswai for her generosity.

Lydia giggles and then rewraps the kaukau and sticks it back on the edge of the coals. She, too, thanks Mataswai, then says something in tok ples that makes Mataswai cover her mouth and giggle also.

"Thank you for showing me your home, Mataswai," I say, smiling at the little brown feet I see dancing behind her mother.

She smiles and nods back. "You are welcome."

"God bless you and your new baby," I say, pointing to her round stomach.

She nods and pats her belly and giggles again.

Then Lydia thanks her, and just as we're about to leave, little Hannah peeks her head out from where she's been lurking behind her mother and with a big smile says, "Hallo!"

"Hello, Hannah," I say. "And good-bye."

"Good-bye," she calls back, happily waving.

"I'm surprised that Mataswai speaks English," I say as we walk through the village. "Is that common?"

"Because Peter's a translation assistant, he's learned English from my parents. And, naturally, he's taught it to his wife and child. If they should ever need to get jobs outside of the village, it would be very useful to know English."

"So they are actually trilingual," I say as we head back to Lydia's house.

"That's right," she says. "Tok ples, pidgin, and English."

"And I'm barely bilingual," I admit. "I mean I've had four years of Spanish, but I'm not sure how well I'd get along in a Spanish-speaking country."

"I know five languages," says Lydia as we walk onto her screened porch and sit down.

"Seriously?"

"Actually, if I really wanted to stretch things, I could say six. When I was little, my brothers taught me some Kauani. I probably wouldn't last very long among people who were fluent in it. But my

German and French aren't too bad. Then there's tok ples and pidgin and English, which makes five."

"Wow, I'm impressed."

She laughs. "Don't be. A lot of people in translation are like this. But it does help me with my job. When you're working for the government, it's a real plus knowing other languages. If I wasn't so interested in medicine, I'd probably consider doing something with languages. But most of all I just want to be a doctor. I don't think there's anything I'd rather do than help people to get well."

"Did you ever consider nursing?"

She sort of turns her nose up now. Then she laughs. "I'm sorry. That probably seems very snooty. And I do have great respect for nurses, but I always wanted to reach higher than that. And so far, all the classes I've taken in college have been aimed toward premed." She sighs. "I suppose I could go for my nursing degree, though."

"No," I say quickly. "Why shouldn't you pursue your dreams? You're obviously smart enough to go to med school." I consider telling her more about our idea for creating a scholarship fund, but after the way her parents reacted, I'm not so sure. I think Sid and I need to discuss it again. We don't want to insult anyone or step over any invisible line. I just wish I understood why they are acting so strangely about this. You'd think parents would be happy to talk about a scholarship for their daughter. Maybe we hurt their pride.

"I guess it's in God's hands," she says. "He knows what's best. Anyway, for now I'm earning pretty good money and saving most of it. That's good."

I nod. "That's really good."

She leans back in the chair and stretches her hands over her head. "But at the moment I'm on holiday. I don't want to even think about work."

"Holiday?" I say. "Is that like vacation?"

"Yes. I have the whole week off. I'll be here until the Bible dedication next weekend. Then it's back to work on Monday."

"That's great," I say. "I'd just assumed you and Peter were going back with us to the airstrip."

"No. But Peter will drive you back to Aiyura for your flight to…wherever it is you and Sid decide to go."

"The Sepik actually sounds pretty interesting."

She nods. "Yes. I haven't been there since I was about ten, but I loved it. I'd love to go back someday."

"Why don't you?"

She shrugs. "I don't know. I guess I could sometime."

"Maybe you could come with us," I suggest. "I mean, if we're really going. It's been so great getting to know you. It'd be cool if you could hang with us awhile longer."

She seems to consider this. "You know, that would be cool."

"What would be cool?" says Sid as she comes out to join us.

So I tell Sid about what I just suggested, and she confirms that we've been officially invited to join the Hanovers in Kauani in the Western Sepik region, and she thinks it's a great idea for Lydia to accompany us. "That is, if your parents are okay with it, Lydia. They might've been looking forward to having you home this week."

Lydia considers this. "Maybe. But if you're really sure you'd like me to go with you, I can ask them. I don't want to be a party crasher."

"We would *love* to have you come with us," says Sid. "In fact, if you don't mind, we could really use your help. First of all with the language, since our pidgin isn't so hot. But I could also talk to you about the AIDS article I'm working on. It sounds like you've learned a lot while volunteering at Saint Luke's, plus teaching your AIDS-awareness classes. I can tell you'd be a great resource, but I haven't had much of a chance to talk with you about all that."

"That's true," says Lydia. "And I'd love to help you in any way I can. I know things won't change in my country without getting more people involved and getting the truth out."

"If you come with us, you'll have to let me cover your expenses since it will be part of my research for the article." Sid shakes her head. "That is, if I ever figure out exactly how I'm going to write this story."

Lydia's eyes light up. "Let me talk to my parents—see what they think of this new development." She heads back into the house, and I tell Sid about my little tour of the village and how I got to meet Peter's wife and see their home.

"I missed out on that?" she says with disappointment. "I've been curious about the living conditions for the villagers."

"I'm sure Mataswai would be happy to show you her house," I tell her. Then I explain how it reminds me of camping.

"So, do you think you could live like that?" she asks.

"For a week or so," I say. "But that's about my max for being a happy camper. About seven days and I'm pretty much craving things like indoor plumbing, a good shower, and a comfortable bed."

After a while Lydia and her parents join us on the porch. Her mom has brought out a pitcher of iced tea and some ginger cookies.

"Lydia said you've invited her to join you this week," says her dad in a careful tone. As he sits down across from Sid, he gives his wife a sideways glance. I can tell by her posture that she's uncomfortable about something, and I have an idea that it's us. Still, I wonder why.

"That's very generous of you," says Mrs. Johnson as she pours a glass of tea and hands it to Sid.

"I hope you don't mind," says Sid. "I mean, that we invited her. But Lydia was so helpful to us at the AIDS clinic in Port Moresby, and that's really why I'm here. My primary interest is in putting together a good, informative article. And she knows so much about the disease as well as the country and the language—she'd be a great asset."

"This must be a fairly expensive piece of journalism that you're writing," says Mr. Johnson.

"Well, I work for a pretty big magazine," admits Sid. Then she explains how John, her editor, spent some time in Papua New Guinea. "Naturally, he okayed the budget for this trip. He felt it would be an important piece. Important enough that he agreed to cover Maddie as my assistant, which has been extremely helpful. Plus, after hearing about the dangers of women traveling alone in this country, well, I'm extra glad to have the company."

"Yes," says Mrs. Johnson eagerly, "that's probably what concerns us the most. Women traveling alone. They can be such an easy target. We really don't like for Lydia to travel alone. We almost always try to make sure she has someone with her on trips."

Lydia kind of makes a face. "Oh, Mom, you know I go by myself a lot of the time. There's no escaping it when I work in the city."

Her mom frowns. "Yes, and that bothers me a lot. You know that."

"But I can't help it," protests Lydia, sounding more like an American than ever now. "I need to work to earn tuition money, and you know I couldn't ask for a better job or a safer place to live in Port Moresby. But it's not like I can have a bodyguard on me twenty-four/seven."

For the first time since we've been here, I sense some family discord, and although I feel bad, I'm sort of relieved too. It's hard to believe any family can get along without a few bumps. It seems only natural for the Johnsons to have theirs. Although I am surprised that Mrs. Johnson is treating Lydia this way. I mean, Lydia is almost twenty-two, and if you ask me, she's a very responsible person. Why are they so worried?

"I suppose Brenda and I are a little overprotective," says Mr. Johnson. "But Lydia is our only daughter. And New Guinea can be a rough country."

"And we'll understand if you're not comfortable letting her come with us," says Sid. I can tell she's getting uneasy now. She's probably wishing I'd never brought up this idea. "Maybe we should've asked you how you felt first."

His brow creases. "Well, to be honest, I really don't have a problem with Lydia joining you." He glances uneasily at his wife. "I actually think you women will be very safe flying into Wewak, staying at the guesthouse, and then heading upriver with one of the Kauani fellows. In fact, I specifically asked Tom to send Micah downriver to get you. He's a very responsible fellow who worked with us as a boy. He's in his thirties now and is still Tom's translation assistant. Like Peter, he also helps to pastor their village church. I can't imagine you being in better hands on the Sepik."

"Micah would bring them upriver?" says Mrs. Johnson in a tone that sounds a bit softer and slightly more positive. "You didn't tell me that, Mark."

He smiles now. "I thought I had. Anyway, I can't imagine Lydia being safer anywhere in this country." He glances at her. "Certainly not in Port Moresby."

Mrs. Johnson sighs. "Yes, I know you're probably right. You're all probably right. I'm sure I must seem very silly." She looks at Lydia now, and I think I see tears in her eyes. "I'm sorry, Lydia. I know I need to stop overprotecting you."

Lydia reaches over and takes her mom's hand. "I understand, Mom. You know I do. But you do have to let go of me. You have to trust God to take care of me."

Mrs. Johnson frowns. "Yes. And I try. But you know…things don't always go the way we think they should."

"Isn't that life?" says Mr. Johnson in a lighter tone. "So, I guess it's settled then. Lydia can go along if she likes. I'll let the Hanovers know they'll be having three guests instead of two. And don't worry. They have plenty of room. It's a bit more like camping than here, but you should be comfortable."

Sid looks a little surprised at how this turned around. I think she must've been ready to give up. I'm so glad the Johnsons changed their minds. I think it'll be great having Lydia along. I also think her mom needs to get beyond this overprotective thing. It's just not healthy. In fact, she reminds me a little of my own mom. But in all fairness, my mom's getting better at it. I mean, she did let me come here, didn't she? Of course, I realize she had no idea what sort of country this really is. For that matter, it seems I haven't totally figured it out either. I mean, I feel very safe here in Lomokako. Well, other than that little earthquake scare this morning. Still, if Mom knew *all* the details… well, she might act just like Lydia's mom.

SIXTEEN

*W*e get ready to leave Lomokako on Monday morning. I feel a little sad as I pack up my things, since I've really enjoyed my visit here. It sort of reminded me of a safe shelter in a storm. But at the same time I'm anxious to see more of this country.

"Thanks so much for your hospitality," Sid tells the Johnsons.

"Yes," I add. "I felt so much at home here. It was really a treat."

Mrs. Johnson takes my hands in hers. "Well, feel free to come back and visit anytime you like."

I laugh. "Yes. Next time I'm in the neighborhood, I'll be sure to stop in."

"Perhaps you'll want to come back with Lydia for the New Testament dedication next weekend," suggests Mr. Johnson. "You'd both be more than welcome."

"Thank you," says Sid. "We'll see how things go this week. And if it seems at all possible, we'll let you know. I assume Lydia knows how to reach you by radio?"

"Of course." Mrs. Johnson nods. "She's known how to work a radio almost as long as she's been talking."

Peter drives us over to Ukarumpa, the mission base for the translators. The plan is to spend one night with some good friends of the

Johnsons there and to fly out of Aiyura in the morning. It's all set up for us. That way we'll get to tour the base, and our flight to the Sepik region will be on Tuesday.

It's almost noon when Peter drives us onto the mission base. Last time we were here, we only saw the airstrip. But today he gives us a short driving tour of what looks like the town *Leave It to Beaver* was filmed in (I used to watch it on Nick at Nite when I was in middle school). He eventually drops us off at a neat little white house down near the river. It even has dark green shutters.

"Conrad and Beth are full-time support personnel," explains Lydia as we get out of the Land Rover. "She teaches preschool, and he's a pilot."

"Hello," calls a petite redhead as she pops out of the front door. "Lydia," she calls out, "so good to see you."

She hugs Lydia and greets Peter, and introductions are made. Peter takes our luggage up to the house, and then we tell him good-bye and thank him for all his help this past week.

"It's been a pleasure," he says with a bright smile.

"Conrad and Beth are my parents' support team," Lydia tells us as we follow Beth into what looks like a typical American home.

"What does that mean?" I ask.

"It means we stay in weekly contact with them by radio," says Beth. "We do their shopping at the grocery store or get them books from the library or whatever they might need. Basically, we're their connection to the outside world, and we try to do what we can to make their life easier."

"And they're great at it too," says Lydia.

"Thanks, sweetie," says Beth. She eyes our luggage, which is piled in their small living room. "Wow, you ladies don't travel too light, do you?"

Sid laughs, then teases me. "I think Maddie overpacked."

"I didn't quite know what to expect," I say in my defense.

"You know, you probably won't be able to take all that on the flight tomorrow. If you like, you could leave some things here and just take what you need."

"And that won't be much," says Lydia as she holds up her own small bag.

Beth pats Lydia on the back. "Lydia's been doing this for a while." Then Beth shows us to a small room that Sid and I will share. "Make yourselves at home."

Beth makes us a nice lunch of soup and sandwiches. Afterward, she gives us a walking tour of Ukarumpa. I'm surprised at how much larger the place seems when you're on foot. And even when we're finished, she tells us we didn't see everything. "There's the primary school and the joinery, where the carpenters work, and some of the newer neighborhoods."

"This really is like a small town," I say as we carry the things we purchased at our last stop, the grocery store, into the house.

"Yes, people are usually surprised at the size of it. You just don't expect to find a place like this in the middle of the remote Eastern Highlands of Papua New Guinea."

"I can see how it would be nice for the translators to have this place," says Sid. "It must give them a feeling of stability while they're out there working in the villages."

Beth nods as she puts groceries away. "Yes. And not having to send kids off to another country for their schooling is huge."

"Speaking of kids," says Lydia as she peeks out the kitchen window, "I think I see yours coming now."

The rest of the day feels so normal that if someone told me I was in the United States, I think I might believe them. Lydia and I ride herd on Beth's kids, and Sid helps Beth fix dinner. Then Conrad comes home, and we all sit down to eat.

"If I hadn't come here and seen this place for myself," I say as we help Beth clean up after dinner, "I never would've believed this is how some missionaries live."

"I have to admit I was surprised too," says Sid. "I always imagine the 'poor missionaries' giving up all the comforts of home. But I think even I could get comfortable here."

Beth laughs. "Yeah, sometimes I almost feel guilty. Like we should have it tougher. And when I try to explain to my friends back in the States that it's not really the sacrifice some people imagine, they usually think I'm playing things down, like I'm some Christian martyr who's willing to suffer in silence. It's really pretty funny."

"Well, you can always tell them that you don't have Starbucks or Nordstrom," I point out. "That might make some people feel sorry for you."

She laughs, then gets a little more serious. "We can't kid ourselves either. There are some very real dangers here." She glances over her shoulder as if to see whether her husband or kids are nearby, which they aren't. "What Conrad does is actually fairly dangerous. Being a JAARS bush pilot in a country like Papua New Guinea doesn't come with any guarantees." She lowers her voice now. "And sometimes he has to fly into some pretty frightening situations."

"Like the time he had to evacuate the Borden family," says Lydia as she rinses a plate and hands it to me. "Their village got into a huge war with a neighboring tribe, and it got so out of hand that people were actually getting killed. Conrad had to fly in by himself during some nasty weather conditions and then airlift out a family of six as well as their translator assistant."

"They couldn't even bring their computers with them," says Beth. "The flight was that full."

"Wow." I finish drying the plate and set it on top of the others.

"At times like that if I didn't have God to lean on, I'd probably totally lose it."

We finish cleaning the kitchen and go to the living room, where Conrad and the kids are horsing around. If Lydia hadn't just told us that story, I'd still be thinking these missionaries have it pretty good. Not that they don't have it good, but I know things aren't usually what they seem on the surface.

The next morning Conrad takes us out to Aiyura with him. He's not the pilot scheduled to fly to Wewak today, so he introduces us to Gary Black from Texas.

"But his friends call him Cowboy," says Conrad, pointing to the straw cowboy hat.

"That's right," says Gary with a heavy Texan drawl. "And sometimes flying in my plane is like riding a bucking bronco in the rodeo."

"Really?" I feel my eyes getting big as I imagine rough turbulence during the trip ahead.

"But it looks right nice out there today," he assures me. "Shouldn't be a problem, little lady."

The flight turns out to be surprisingly smooth. Cowboy even points out the highest peak in New Guinea, Mount Wilhelm.

"Sometimes there's snow on top," says Lydia, "but I don't see any today."

"We have some good-sized mountains where we're from," I tell them. "But Mount Wilhelm is taller than our tallest mountain."

"If I were younger, I might consider trying to climb it," says Cowboy. "Some of my pilot buddies have done it. But they did it when they were young bucks. I'm a little long in the tooth for that sort of thing."

"I know you haven't been in New Guinea for too long," says Lydia. "What did you do before you came here?"

"I flew in South America. Now, we're talking about exciting stuff down there. A little too exciting."

"How's that?" I ask.

"Well, I flew in Colombia for many years." He slowly shakes his head. "Too many drug wars and too much political craziness going on in that country. We finally had to shut JAARS down completely. Too risky."

"Back in the nineties I did a story on missionaries who'd been kidnapped in Colombia," says Sid. "It was a very sad situation."

He nods. "Yeah, places like that make Papua New Guinea look like a walk in the park."

"Is that the Sepik?" asks Lydia, pointing below us to what looks like a length of silver chain surrounded by green.

"Good spotting, Lydia!"

Within minutes Cowboy makes a sharp left turn, and we follow the silver snaking river for a while. "And there's Wewak, right where she's supposed to be," he says as we begin to descend. Once again the airstrip looks awfully small to me from up here, but before long we land on it and come to a full stop before we reach the end.

As soon as the doors open, I can feel that moist, tropical heat flooding in, and I know we're not in the highlands anymore. Several nationals come over to greet us and begin unloading the plane. Cowboy hands us our carry-on bags and thanks us for flying with him.

"Thank you," says Sid. "That was a very nice flight." Then we walk over to a building, which Cowboy explains is the guesthouse and where, according to Lydia, they will be expecting us for lunch.

"Apinun, Missis," calls a man who's quickly approaching us and waving with enthusiasm. "Nem bilong mi Micah. Yu stap gut?" He smiles brightly as he reaches for my carry-on bag. "Mi helpim yu."

Without releasing my bag, I glance at Sid, hoping for some direction, but she looks totally blank. Then we both turn to Lydia to find that she has a slightly puzzled expression, as if she's not too sure either. So she begins to speak politely to him in pidgin. I try to follow, and I get the sense that she's questioning him, but then their conversation starts going way too fast. Judging by Lydia's tone of voice, I think she's getting really mad at him. Finally she raises her arms and yells at him, and he turns and runs away, straight into the trees growing alongside the airstrip.

"What just happened?" asks Sid as Lydia takes us both by the arms and hurries us over to the guesthouse.

"That man was *not* Micah," gasps Lydia.

"How do you know?" asks Sid. "It sounded like he said he was Micah."

"I know. And I know it must seem strange," she admits as we're going up the steps to the guesthouse, which overlooks the river. "To be honest, I haven't seen Micah in years, not since I was a little girl. I'm sure I wouldn't recognize him today. But something inside me made me suspicious. And when I asked him some questions about the Hanovers and then about my own parents, he didn't have the right answers. Not even close."

"Who do you think he was?" I ask. "And how did he know where to meet us and to use Micah's name?"

She shakes her head. "I don't know. But I do know he was up to no good."

"Seriously?" Sid turns and looks back as if she expects to see the impostor again, but he's long gone now. "Do you think he was going to rob us?"

"I think it's a possibility."

"What if we'd gone with him?" I say, feeling my knees get a little wobbly at the thought.

Lydia sighs. "I don't know."

"Wow."

"Should we report this?" asks Sid.

"We'll tell the guesthouse people," says Lydia. "But I doubt it will do much good to contact the police."

"Man, am I glad you're with us," I say as we go inside.

"I'm glad too," she says. Then she smiles. "I think God wanted me to come."

Sid gives Lydia a little sideways hug. "Maybe you're our angel, Lydia."

We tell the woman who's in charge of the guesthouse about what just happened on the airstrip.

"We've had trouble like that from time to time," she says in a heavy Australian accent, "but not anything recently."

"I wonder how this man knew to use Micah's name," Sid says.

The woman frowns. "Well, Micah arrived about an hour ago. He was fueling up his motor down at the dock. I suspect that rascal overheard him talking to someone down there. Or perhaps someone greeted Micah by name. I'll tell you this much, if a rascal is up to no good, he will find clever ways of procuring information."

"Well, thankfully, Lydia figured it out," I tell her.

"Good girl," says the woman. "Unfortunately, you can't be too careful these days."

SEVENTEEN

*A*fter lunch we meet the real Micah down at the dock. I can tell that Lydia isn't the least bit worried, but it's reassuring that she takes the time to quickly quiz him just the same. He looks a little confused, but he politely answers her questions.

"He's the real deal," she tells us. "I'll explain to him why I was grilling him just now." So she turns and, speaking in pidgin, tells him what I assume is our little story.

Micah nods with concern in his eyes. Then he says something, which she translates back to us.

"Micah says there *was* a stranger hanging around the dock this morning. But he was friendly, and Micah, being a good Christian man, spoke to him. He's very sorry now."

"Well, I guess we all learned a lesson today," says Sid.

Then Micah helps us onto a motorboat, and once we're seated, he starts the engine, and we are on our way.

"It's about three hours from here," says Lydia. "Relax and enjoy the ride."

And it is an enjoyable ride. Even though it's hot, we sit under the shade of the awning, and the wind rushing by as we move upriver is refreshing. I had no idea that our trip to the Sepik would include an enjoyable boat ride like this.

"Look," says Lydia, pointing to what looks like a partially submerged log, "a crocodile!"

I squint at the brownish thing, and then Micah slows the boat down and steers closer to it. When we're about ten feet away, the object suddenly moves, and with a whip of its tail, it dives under the water and disappears. Then Micah laughs and takes off again.

"That *was* a crocodile!" I exclaim, my heart pounding with excitement.

"We disturbed his nap," says Lydia.

"Are we in any danger out here?" I ask.

"No. They're probably more afraid of us than we are of them."

We're going by what appears to be a village now, with houses on tall stilts not far from the river's edge. Some young children with very little clothing on are playing in the water, taking turns jumping into the river and climbing out again. But when they see us, they stop and yell and wave.

"Aren't they worried about the crocodiles?" I ask.

"They're careful," says Lydia. "They know this time of day is pretty safe since *puk-puks* are nocturnal."

"Puk-puks?"

"Pidgin for 'crocodiles.'"

"Watch out for the puk-puks," I yell out to the kids. Of course, this makes them shriek and laugh, and then they start pushing each other toward the water.

We also see people traveling in long dugout canoes. For the most part they seem to be women, and I notice they have a trail of smoke coming from the back of their canoes. I ask Lydia why that is.

"The women take the canoes to go work in their gardens. Some gardens are far away from the village. They take a pot with some coals along with them so they can use it to cook lunch and then to start their cooking fire when they get home. It saves time."

"And matches?"

She laughs. "It's so damp here in the Sepik that matches aren't all that useful. And lighters run out after a while. I think their traditional ways are probably still pretty handy."

"Do they make their canoes?" I ask.

"Yes. They're always on the lookout for a good tree. When they find one that's big and straight and solid and close to the river, they'll cut it down and float it back to their village."

"How do they hollow it out?"

"They have some hand tools," she says. "And they use fire to burn away the wood they want to remove. It takes weeks of hard work, but they eventually get it all hollowed out, and then they seal the outside of the wood with fire and heat. That's why they look so black and sooty."

We spot a few more crocodiles, or puk-puks. I take lots of photos and enjoy all the passing scenery while Sid asks Lydia a lot of questions and takes some notes. Then, as our boat is going through what seems like acres and acres of sugarcane growing right there in the water, a beautiful white crane flies in front of us, almost as if it's leading us through this maze. To be honest, I wonder if we might possibly be lost, but eventually we're out on the river again. Around four o'clock, we approach what appears to be a fairly large village.

"This is it," says Lydia as Micah eases the boat alongside a sturdy dock.

"Hello, ladies," calls a middle-aged white man who's coming down the steps onto the dock. "Welcome to Kauani." He extends a hand to help us out of the boat as Micah ties it up. Lydia introduces us to Tom Hanover, and we report on our trip. Then Micah hands us our bags, and Tom helps Micah remove the outboard motor from the boat.

"We'll just be a minute," he tells us. "If we don't lock this thing up, it'll sprout legs and walk away before morning."

Lydia laughs. "Yes. My dad said that happened to him once."

"Once is more than enough," calls Tom as he and Micah lug the heavy motor to a shed at the end of the dock. They put it inside and then padlock the door.

"All right," says Tom. "Donna can't wait to see you ladies." He points up the steps. "To the house."

Lydia leads the way, and we follow.

"The river is usually low this time of year," he tells us when we get to the landing on top. "We're about ten feet above the river here, but sometimes during the big rains, the water will come up quite high."

"And see those houses?" says Lydia, pointing to brown structures that resemble storks on their tall, stiltlike legs. "Sometimes the water is right beneath them. It completely surrounds them."

"So how do the people get around?" I ask.

"They just tie their canoes up to the door," explains Tom. "Pretty convenient, huh?"

"That'd be cool," I say. "Climb out of your house and hop right into your boat."

"What about the crocodiles?" asks Sid. "Can they swim up and get into the houses then?"

Tom laughs. "Well, I've never heard of that happening, but you never know."

"Hello," calls a woman from a large house that's also built on stilts but sits on top of a knoll. It's much bigger than what I assume are the village houses down below. And unlike the village houses, this one has a corrugated metal roof and what I'm sure must be a water tank off to one side.

"Company's here," says Tom, taking a moment to introduce us. "And if you ladies will excuse me now, I have a few things to take care of before dinnertime."

Donna waves him away as we come up the stairs. "We won't even know you're gone, honey."

Once we're inside the house, I see that it's like a giant screened box. The view of the river and palm trees and village houses off to one side is stunning. Tall palm trees bend toward the blue water. It's like something you'd see on a postcard.

"What a gorgeous view," I say as I walk around, looking up and down the river. "And what a fantastic location for a house!"

Lydia chuckles.

"Why is that funny?" I ask her.

"Because Lydia knows the history of this house," says Donna.

"What's the history of this house?" asks Sid.

"Actually, it's the history of this land," explains Donna as she motions for us to sit down in the wicker furniture that's comfortably arranged by the window with the best view. "The original translators got a real deal on it."

"You have to *buy* the land to build your house on?" I say. "Even when you come here to help these people?"

"In most cases you do. Sometimes a village is willing to give land in exchange for things like schools and medicine—or at least they used to be—but most of them expect cold, hard cash in return for land nowadays."

"So why was this land such a good deal?" asks Sid as she pulls out a small notebook. "It seems like a prime piece of property."

Donna nods. "That's what we think too. But when the first translators came here, no one in the village wanted them to stay. Especially the headman."

"Headman?" I repeat.

"He's like the chief or the mayor or, in some cases, the dictator. Anyway, this headman did not want missionaries of any kind in his village. But they persisted. And fortunately for the missionaries, there were a few people who wanted them to stay. But the headman decided to play a trick on the translators by offering them this piece of property."

"How could that possibly be a trick?" I ask, gazing out at the peaceful view.

"Because this was the site of an ancient burial ground," she explains. "And everyone believed it was haunted. No person in their right mind would ever want to live here."

I glance around the room, almost expecting to see a ghost, which I know is ridiculous.

"But the translators said they weren't afraid, and they bought the land and started to build their house." Donna sighs. "Of course, they did end up having some problems."

Lydia nods. "Yes. The husband got a puncture wound in his foot and came down with tetanus before the house was finished."

"Naturally, the headman claimed it happened because the spirits were mad."

"The couple had to leave so he could get treatment," says Lydia, "but then they came back and finished the house."

"The headman was still certain the spirits would drive the couple away," continues Donna. "And it wasn't long before the wife got sick. And, once again, they had to leave for medical treatment."

"It turned out to be just appendicitis," explains Lydia.

"However, appendicitis out here can be lethal," says Donna. "Then they made it for about six years without any serious health problems."

"Of course, during that whole time, the headman and his buddies did everything they could think of to scare this couple away," says Lydia.

"Fortunately, none of it worked," adds Donna. "And to the headman's great angst, the people in the village really began to love this couple. They figured if they'd survived that long, then the spirits must like them—or perhaps the spirits had sent them. It helped matters that the wife was a nurse. She saved many lives here just by using the simplest of medical practices."

"So what went wrong?" I ask, knowing the Johnsons had eventually taken over here.

"They went back to the States on furlough," says Donna. "The woman had been having stomachaches, and when she was checked, they found out she had pancreatic cancer."

"Ugh." Sid shakes her head. "I've heard that's bad."

Donna nods. "They never made it back."

"That must've made the headman happy."

"Oh, I'm sure he partied for days when they left and didn't come back."

"But then my parents showed up," says Lydia proudly. "Of course, they weren't my parents then. But they never had any serious health problems at all while they lived here."

"It wasn't easy for the Johnsons though," says Donna. "It's like they had to start over with the people. And even to this day there are a few old-timers who think that the Johnsons did something bad to the original couple." She kind of laughs. "For some reason they took to us. We've made lots of good friends in the village."

"What about the headman?" I ask.

"Oh, he's long gone. His son is headman now, and he's getting old."

"How old is old?" asks Sid.

"The average life expectancy in New Guinea varies, based on where you live. Around here, we think it's about fifty to fifty-five."

Sid gulps. "That puts me way over the hill."

Donna makes a face. "Hey, we know how you feel. But those numbers only apply to the locals. And they're actually better now than they were, say, thirty years ago. It has to do with nutrition and medicine—you know, the basics."

Then Sid explains what brought us to New Guinea and about the article she's working on. "So, how is it out here?" she asks. "Do you ever see any incidents of AIDS?"

"Do we see it?" repeats Donna as if she's considering her answer. "We're pretty sure we've seen it. At least we suspected it. But it's not something people will talk about openly. We felt certain that one of our villagers had contracted the disease, and there was plenty of gossip regarding his infidelities. But even when Tom took him aside and had a private conversation, the man denied everything. Of course, we all knew he'd been downriver a lot, visiting other villages, and the rumor was that he had several women friends. He'd bragged about it to some of the men, who then reported it to Tom."

"What happened to him?" asks Sid.

"He just got sicker and sicker and eventually died of what was called pneumonia, but I'm fairly certain it was simply a complication of AIDS."

"What about his wife?" I ask.

"She died recently, just a couple of years after his death. Similar thing: deteriorating health, open sores, finally what appeared to be pneumonia. Naturally, there was some gossip about it going around the village at the time. But the assumption was that someone had worked poison on her."

"What does that mean?" asks Sid.

"The practice is tied in with spiritual beliefs that date back to their ancestors hundreds of years ago. Even the strongest Christians in our village still have a hard time getting completely away from the pull of those beliefs—the ancient ties are strong. But people in our village started saying that the wife must've worked poison on her husband after finding out about his infidelities. This was their explanation for how he died. And for revenge, his spirit had returned from the dead to work poison on her. A payback. End of story."

"In a way, that's true," I say. Of course, now they all look at me like I'm nuts. "I mean, the husband did sort of 'work poison' on his wife by infecting her with HIV."

"I never thought of it quite like that," says Donna. "But it does make sense."

"She's exactly right," says Lydia in a serious tone. "HIV is a very real form of poison." She pauses as if really considering this theory. "If you think about it, my people have been talking about *poison,* fearing *poison,* even prophetically predicting *poison* for generations, and now it's as if it's arrived in the form of HIV—and that *poison* is spreading like wildfire."

"That's so weird," says Donna. "But I think you've hit the nail on the head, Lydia."

"What a great angle for my story," says Sid as she writes down more notes. "I mean, it's tragic and horrible, but connecting AIDS, even metaphorically, with the old form of spirit poison, that's profound." She holds up her already-filled small notebook. "Oh, I wish I'd brought my laptop along."

"We have more paper," offers Donna, quickly getting up and

going over to a desk. She pulls out a tablet and hands it to Sid. "Here, write that down before we forget what we were talking about. In the meantime, I'd better start dinner."

"Would you like some help?" I stand up.

"Yes," says Lydia. "I can help too."

"No," says Sid suddenly. "Let Maddie help. I need you to come over here and talk to me about this some more, Lydia. I think you've got some amazing insights that the rest of us might be missing."

"Thanks," Donna says to me. "I'd love some help."

As I cut up a pineapple, I try not to feel too dismissed by my aunt just now. I mean it's totally cool that Lydia has made this poison connection with AIDS. But, in all fairness, I brought it up first. Okay, I tell myself, don't be so childish. It doesn't matter who thought of it first. The important thing is that Sid has a great angle for her article now. What difference does it make if she credits Lydia with this instead of me? In other words, get over it, Maddie! Grow up!

EIGHTEEN

*D*o you ever feel as if you're in fishbowl up here?" asks Sid after dinner. We're sitting in the living room area, and it's dark out now. What was a beautiful view of river, sky, and palm trees earlier is now a sea of black.

"I think it bothered us at first," admits Donna, "but we got used to it."

"And living out in the open like this seems to reassure our neighbors," says Tom. "Shows them we're not up to something."

"Of course, the bedrooms have more privacy," says Donna. "The screens don't start until five feet up. So people outside might be able to see your head if they happened to be standing in the right spot, but that's about it. And the openness helps to keep the air flowing through and allows it to cool down in here at night."

"Do you think the people watch you?" I ask as I try to peer through the screen, still seeing nothing but inky darkness.

"Not usually," says Tom. Then he chuckles. "But since we have guests, it's possible."

Sid tells them a bit more about her job as a journalist and the project she's working on now. And Tom tells her about a couple of AIDS cases he's heard about here in the Sepik River region. "I don't think it's common," he says, "but I have to admit being surprised that it made it here at all. Of course, infidelity is an issue in this culture. Certainly not as bad as in the States, since I've heard that nearly half of American marriages are affected by it. Here it's more the exception, but we do have at least two cases in our village right now. In fact, some of the worst fights we've seen have been between women who aren't happy sharing the same man."

"Yes," says Donna, "it can get ugly. The goal of the jealous wife is usually to deform the other woman's face."

"So when we see a woman with scars on her face…"

"Yes, it can mean that she's been the *other* woman."

"Or simply accused of being her," adds Tom.

Then Sid tells Tom about the theory of AIDS being like poison, and he listens with interest, nodding and taking it in.

"I can see the correlation," he says. "Poison in this culture is related to someone who's done something bad or is associated with someone who's done something bad. And it results in sickness and sometimes even death."

Sid grabs the tablet and starts taking notes again. "So clarify this for me, please. Does that mean a person who believes a spirit has worked poison on him, as you say, will get physically ill?"

"Yes, it's rather mysterious. Some experts think it's totally psychosomatic and that because a person believes he's been poisoned, he will exhibit the symptoms. Others think that the affected person probably already had a virus or infection, but combine that with the poison theory, and he is rendered even more vulnerable."

"And there have been some strange stories," says Lydia. "A man in our village had been out walking at night. He said a spirit accosted him and put arrows in his feet. And when his swollen, aching feet were examined, there were actual slivers of bamboo or wood that had to be removed. He got a terrible infection, and my parents eventually had him flown out to get more medical treatment."

"You don't suppose he simply walked on something like thorns, do you?" asks Sid.

"I don't know." Lydia shakes her head. "I wasn't very old at the time, but I do remember being spooked by it."

"We've had similar stories here," says Donna. "It sort of defies scientific explanation. Of course, the way the stories get told and retold, it's hard to say what's really true sometimes."

"But connecting AIDS with poison is an interesting way of looking at it," says Tom. "And it might be a way to educate people in this country, to make them respect that AIDS is a very real thing. If nothing else, it's a good attention getter."

"Well, it does give an interesting twist to my article," says Sid. "I'm so glad that Lydia helped us to make this connection."

Lydia looks a bit uncomfortable now, and I wonder if she feels bad for taking all the credit for this idea. But then she says she's tired and wants to turn in. Donna has already shown us where we'll be sleeping. Sid and I are sharing what was their daughter's room. And Lydia gets a small room with a bunk that doubles as an office.

We visit for another hour, but it seems we're all pretty weary, and before long we call it a night. The bathroom facilities are a bit more primitive here. They have only a bucket shower. But, as Donna pointed out, at least they have an indoor toilet now. Apparently that wasn't always the case. And they still have the outhouse for emergencies, although she warned me that snakes or spiders could be out there and I should "be careful." I'm thinking it'll have to be a major emergency for me to ever use the outhouse, thank you very much.

"I've never slept under a mosquito net before," I tell Sid. "How about you?"

"Oh, sure," she says as she pulls up the net and crawls into bed.

"It's kind of cool."

"Yeah," she says sleepily. "Just don't forget to tuck it in securely around the mattress in the morning. Otherwise, you might go to bed and find that something has sneaked in. Donna told me that once in a while a snake will slip into the house, and her son, Aaron, found one in his bed one night."

"That's a lovely thought," I say, going around the entire bed to check that my net is tucked in on all sides. It looks secure. Then I glance at the light that's on the table between our two beds. "How do you turn off the light once you're in bed?"

She sort of laughs. "You turn it off *first*," she says. "Then get in bed."

"Oh." So I turn off the light and then stumble around in the darkness trying to get into my mosquito netting. It's a trick to get it tucked back around the mattress so that nothing can sneak in during the night. That comment about the snake in the bed was pretty unnerving.

I lie there in the darkness, and before long I can tell that Sid's asleep. But I'm having a little problem. It's like I'm afraid to stretch my feet to the foot of the bed because I keep imagining a snake down there. I mean, how do I know this mosquito netting has been securely tucked around this bed for however long since someone last slept here? What if it has been open and a snake slithered in? The image of a sleeping snake curled at the end of my bed is so creepy that I'm sure I won't be able to go to sleep now. Still, I hate getting out and turning on the light and making noise. I timidly stretch one foot down a few more inches, holding my breath and expecting some serpentlike thing to sink its sharp teeth into my toe. Then I pull my foot back up and curl into a ball. I know this is perfectly ridiculous. There's probably not a snake in my bed. And yet I cannot shake that image.

Finally I can stand it no longer. I pull the mosquito netting out and leap out of my bed and turn on the light.

"What's wrong?" demands Sid, blinking in the bright light. "Another earthquake?"

"I'm sorry," I tell her. "I thought something was in my bed."

"Oh."

So I pull back the top sheet and lightweight blanket and carefully examine every square inch of the bed. I poke around and even look under the bottom sheet and in the pillowcase.

"Anything there?" she asks sleepily.

"No," I admit as I start putting my bed back together and retucking the netting into place.

"Think you can sleep now?" she asks.

"Yes," I say as I turn off the light. "Sorry about that."

She just makes a groaning sound and rolls over. Still, I'm glad I checked. Now I can relax and sleep in peace. And before long I hear Sid's even breathing that tells me she has gone back to sleep. Hopefully, she won't remember my paranoia in the morning. I take a deep breath and roll over on my side so that I'm facing the wall where the screen begins partway up. But I see the weirdest thing! In fact, I'm pretty sure I'm hallucinating. I sit up and blink my eyes as I look out the upper screen at what appear to be hundreds of tiny lights, slightly flickering. What is going on? I clear my throat, hoping I'll wake Sid again. But she just keeps sleeping. I blink again and look at the lights, wondering if it's some kind of alien spaceship out there, hovering behind the house. Then I remember how this house is built on an old burial ground, and I wonder if there really are some unhappy spirits gathering tonight. I know it's crazy, and I know my imagination needs to settle down, but I cannot for the life of me figure out what is going on outside. It's so strange.

I don't know how long I sit there in bed, afraid to move, afraid to say anything, just staring at these lights. And I begin to wonder if they're hypnotizing me, getting me into their power. Maybe they'll work poison on me and I'll get sick and die in the morning. Finally I can't stand it, and I'm afraid I'm going to scream. But instead, I close my eyes and begin to pray. I beg God to protect me—from whatever this thing is, even if it's just my own overactive imagination. I sit there and pray for a long time. I'm about to open my eyes again to see if that weird phenomenon is still there, but I don't. I decide that I don't want to know. Instead, I will focus on God. I will imagine his protection wrapping around me just like this mosquito net. And then I make myself lie down. I take a deep breath, and I remind myself of the Bible verse that says to take every thought captive to Jesus. And that's what I do. Only by the grace of God I'm sure, I finally go to sleep and do not wake up until morning.

Sid is already up, her bed neatly made and the mosquito net securely in place. I can hear voices in the house, and I know I must look like the lazy one. So I hurry and get up and dress in the only other outfit I have to wear, since we packed ultralight. Then I pull my hair back into a ponytail and go out to where they're just setting the table for breakfast.

"Sorry I slept in," I say.

"No worries," says Donna. "I'm glad you slept well."

I consider this, remembering what I saw last night or what I think I saw, and try to decide whether I want to risk sounding totally ridiculous by mentioning it. Finally I decide, *What does it matter if I look ridiculous?*

"Uh, I saw something weird last night," I begin in an unsteady voice.

Well, this gets everyone's attention, and they turn and look at me with curiosity. "What?" asks Donna.

"I know it might be my imagination," I admit, "but it looked so real…"

"What was it?" demands Sid with a concerned look. I think she's worried that I'm losing it.

"Well, I looked out the screen, and it was like there were a hundred tiny lights out there." Then I start talking fast. "They were glimmering in the dark, and it was so weird I almost thought it was aliens or spirits or something, but I told myself it was just my imagination going nuts on me, and then I had to pray, I mean really pray, so I could settle down and go to sleep. But then I did. Go to sleep, I mean. I guess I was sort of hallucinating, huh?"

Tom and Donna start laughing. But Sid looks slightly terrified, and Lydia is simply smiling.

"I saw it too," says Lydia.

"You did?" Okay, now I want to hug her. "Really? I'm not going crazy?"

"No," gasps Donna, trying to catch her breath from laughing so hard.

"It was the fireflies," says Tom.

"Fireflies?"

"Yes," says Donna. "They love that tree, and sometimes they come from all over and meet there, covering it like a Christmas tree. I'm not sure why. But isn't it a beautiful sight?"

I blink. "Yeah," I admit, "it really was. Except that it sort of scared me."

"I can understand that," says Donna. "After the things we'd been talking about and being in a strange place, it would be pretty unsettling."

Now I smile. "Well, I feel kind of silly, but I feel better too. I mean, I'm glad I didn't imagine it."

"Why didn't you wake me up?" asks Sid. "I would've liked to see it too."

I laugh now. "After I woke you up thinking there was a snake in my bed?"

"There was a snake in your bed?" asks Donna with a horrified look.

"No," I say quickly. "I just thought there was. I kind of imagined it. And that's probably why I thought I imagined the firefly thing."

"Well, I wish you'd awakened me," says Sid. "It sounds amazing."

"It was," I tell her. "But you were sound asleep."

After breakfast, Donna invites Sid and me to tour the village. Lydia is into a book that Donna loaned her, and since she's seen the village before, she stays behind. "I'm on holiday," she reminds us with a smile.

"That's right," says Sid. "You should be able to do what you want."

Donna guides us through the quiet village, which seems mostly empty except for elderly people, small children, and an occasional dog. She explains that it's because the women are working in their gardens, and the men are fishing or hunting or hiding out in the "men's house."

"What's the men's house?" I ask.

She takes us over by the river and points to a jutting piece of land where a long, rectangular building is situated by itself. The sides are open like the church back in Lomokako, and sure enough we spot about a dozen men sitting over there and a trail of smoke coming out.

"They go there to smoke their pipes and gossip," says Donna. "Like a men's club in the States."

Sid laughs. "Some things just seem universal."

Then Donna takes us into a house where she checks on the health of an old woman. The houses in Kauani are similar to Lomokako as far as building materials go, but otherwise they're quite different. First of all, they're built up high, and you have to climb a steep ladder to get inside, which makes me wonder how some of these elderly people get up them. It seems a bit precarious to me, and I can tell Sid isn't comfortable. Of course, I know these ladders get much shorter during the wet season when the river rises and the people can tie their canoes to the door.

Their houses are square instead of round, and their roofs are a lot higher too. I suppose that helps the air circulate and keeps the place cooler, since it's much warmer here in the lowlands. But, like the Lomokako house I visited, this one also has a cooking fire in the center. Lined with stone and dirt, it somehow manages to burn without burning down the house, which I'm guessing would be highly combustible.

Donna introduces us to the old woman and gives her some medicine and water, then helps her to lie back down. The woman gives us a weak and toothless smile, then closes her eyes.

"She's not long for this world," says Donna. "But she's a Christian, and she's ready to go."

As we're leaving, I notice some green wrapped bundles on the edges of the smoldering fire. "Is that kaukau?" I ask, remembering the sample I had back in Lomokako.

"No, that's *saksak*."

Sid's confused now. "What are you two talking about?" So I explain about kaukau and how I sampled it.

"Would you like to sample some saksak?" asks Donna.

"No, thank you," I say quickly. "But maybe Sid would."

Sid holds up her hands. "I pass. But what is it?"

"It's related to tapioca," explains Donna. "It's kind of thick and pasty. But they don't sweeten it. They just let it smoke on the fires, and when it's done, it's similar to thick mashed potatoes with no seasoning."

"Sounds yummy," says Sid.

"Would you like to see how they make it?" asks Donna. "It's pretty interesting."

We agree and leave the house, climbing back down the tall ladder. Below, she takes us over to where several women are working around a tree that's been cut down. At first I think they might be making a canoe, but then Donna explains.

"It's a palm tree called nipa. First they cut one down, then they split it open with an ax and begin to remove that fibrous material you see there." She points to some light brown stuff that looks like straw. "Once that's removed, it's washed in that vat." She points to where another woman is pouring water over the fiber and pounding on it— smashing and pounding again and again. Then she releases the water, which has turned a whitish color, by opening a chute, and it's collected in a wooden bowl.

"They boil this liquid over here," says Donna as she takes us to where the third woman is stirring a mixture in a large metal pot over a fire. The contents look like a thick, pale gray pudding. "And when it's ready, they wrap it in the banana leaves to smoke over their fires."

"How did they ever come up with this process?" I ask. "I mean, what made them think they could chop down a palm tree, smash up the fiber, turn it into water, and cook it into something edible?"

Donna laughs. "It is rather odd, isn't it? Maybe God showed their ancestors how."

I consider this possibility as we head back to the house to make lunch. If you think about it, it's pretty amazing that humans have figured out so many things—ways to survive, to make food, to create medicine, whatever. Maybe God really did show them.

NINETEEN

*W*ould you girls like to take a canoe out?" asks Donna after we clean up the lunch dishes. "We have one you can use to tool around in if you want."

"That sounds great," says Lydia. "As good as that book is, I think I'm ready to go out and get some fresh air and exercise now."

"The canoe is down at the dock," says Donna, "over behind the boathouse shed."

So Lydia and I go down to the dock and untie the canoe. I ask Lydia if she knows anything about canoeing, and she assures me she's had some experience.

"I've only been in a canoe a couple of times," I admit, "but I do know they're tippy."

Lydia finds some paddles hanging on the boathouse, and we line the canoe up with the dock and carefully get in. I follow her example by grasping both sides of the canoe and placing first one foot in the center and then the other. To my surprise it feels fairly sturdy. Unlike the aluminum canoes I've been in, this one is solid and heavy and doesn't rock and roll as much.

"Ready?" she asks as she lets go of the dock and gives us a gentle push into the river.

"Nice launch," I say as I dip my paddle into the water and try a tentative stroke.

It takes us a few minutes to get a rhythm to our paddling, but soon we get it down, and before long we're going upriver at a pretty good pace.

"This is fun," I tell her.

"So peaceful," she says, leaning back to look at the blue sky above us.

The water's not moving very fast, but we can tell it takes more paddling to go against the current, so we decide to keep going upriver. "Then if we get tired, we can just let the river push us back to Kauani," says Lydia.

We see women in canoes, either alone or in pairs, with their little cook fires in the rear and a trail of lazy smoke following them as they paddle back to the village. I spot some baskets with what looks like produce, I'm guessing from their gardens, probably for tonight's dinner.

"This isn't such a bad way to live," I say.

"Not at all," she agrees. "For the most part anyway. The biggest challenge of tribal life is the lack of good medical care and treatment. The worst threat for these people is getting sick."

I nod. "And I'm sure the tropical climate doesn't help that much. Still, it's a beautiful place to live."

"Yes. I like the Sepik region."

"I really like where your family lives too," I say. "In fact, if I had to pick one over the other, I'd go for Lomokako in a heartbeat."

She smiles. "You would?"

I nod. "Yes. I felt totally at home there."

"You did?" She seems genuinely surprised by this.

"Yes," I tell her. "Very much so. In fact, your parents remind me a lot of my own parents. Your mom and my mom could almost be related—maybe they were twins separated at birth."

"You mean they look alike?"

I consider this. "Well, not exactly. But they act alike."

She frowns now. "How's that?"

"Well…" Now I don't want to offend her, but she seems genuinely curious. "I guess it was the way your mom was being so protective of you—you know, when you were going to come here with us." I smile and shrug. "That's exactly like something my mom would do too."

She nods. "Well, to be fair, my mom wasn't always like that. She used to let me have lots and lots of freedom, just coming and going without her asking any questions. She didn't worry at all."

This surprises me. I mean, that sounds like a totally cool mom. Like my friend Katie's mom. She's so laid back that I've always been slightly envious. "So why did your mom change?"

We've gone quite a ways now, and I think we got tired simultaneously. Our paddles are balanced across the top of the canoe, and we're just sitting, drifting along as we take a little break, allowing the slow current to move us back downriver.

"Oh, it's a long story."

"I have time." I smile and wait.

But her brow is creased, and she seems troubled now. Suddenly I wonder if I'm being too nosy. Maybe something happened to her mom that's none of my business.

"I'm sorry," I say quickly. "I mean, maybe it's personal. I didn't mean to be so—"

"No, it's okay," she says. "And, yes, it is personal, but I've been thinking I should tell you anyway."

Now I'm remembering the concerns I had for Lydia when we were in her village, like the possibility that her parents were doing the traditional New Guinean thing and setting her up with a husband, asking for a bride price. Maybe she was already spoken for, and they were trying to protect her for her betrothed. Okay, I suppose that seems crazy and overly dramatic, but after some of the things I've seen and read about this totally different culture, well, you just never know. Plus, there's definitely something about her relationship with her parents, particularly with her mom, that feels strange to me. Even Sid noticed it. But we assumed Mrs. Johnson was just extremely protective. Like my mom times ten.

"You see, my brothers and I had always been raised to be independent," she begins. "It's that way with a lot of kids whose parents are translators. We had to learn to come and go and take care of ourselves at a fairly young age. And it was never a problem. Like I told you, we were sent to live on the mission base and attend school there. And, sure, it was a little hard in the beginning, but I got used to it.

"Then, after graduation, my brothers and I, one by one, went to the States for our first two years of college with paid tuition. I was seventeen when I graduated, and I couldn't wait to go to Oregon and start my 'grownup' life. I stayed with my mom's relatives, just like my brothers had done during their first year. And even though it was a challenge to adjust to American culture, I sort of got the hang of it. I wanted to follow my brothers' examples, and I got good grades and stayed out of trouble. But somehow I just didn't fit in as well as they had. Maybe it was my skin color, or maybe it was genetic roots back here.

"My brothers both got jobs after the first two years to earn more tuition money, and they continued their education. Jeremy graduated a couple of years ago and Caleb just last June. They both seem very settled. In fact, Caleb just got engaged."

"But you came back here?"

She nods. "Yes. I finished my two years with a very respectable grade-point average, but I just couldn't acclimate. I think I was home-sick. And perhaps that's because I am New Guinean. In fact, right before coming home I chose to return to my birth name, Obuti. I decided to come back to my homeland and find a good job in Port Moresby. I suppose in some ways, I felt a little lost right then. I didn't really fit into American culture, and I didn't really fit in here either. But I thought I could find my place better in my own country."

I nod. "That makes sense."

"It did to me too. In fact, I was so glad to get back here that I told myself I'd never leave again. I really believed somehow I would make my own way here. I wasn't sure if I'd return to college or try to settle into some work I enjoyed. And I suppose I sort of distanced myself from my parents just then—I think I wanted to show them I could make it on my own."

"And?"

"Well, because of my knowledge of languages, I easily got a job with the government. I shared a flat with another girl who worked in the same place. Our flat wasn't in such a great part of town, but it didn't concern me since the rent was affordable, which meant I could save more." She sighs. "And to be honest, I wasn't being very careful. In fact, I'd been more careful while living in Portland than I was when I returned to my homeland. I was so happy to be back home that I think I got a false sense of security here."

I nod but suddenly feel worried about where this story is going. "I can understand how that would happen," I tell her. "I mean I've been hypercautious here in your country. And I'm sure I'll completely let my guard down at home. But I realize that's not so smart either. Especially if you're in a big city."

"That's true." She looks directly at me now. "Something happened. Something that changed everything."

I wait for her to continue, and I can tell by her eyes that it's not easy to tell this story.

"I was coming home from work one night. I'd stayed later than usual, and it was already dark. I should've called for a taxi, but I didn't want to waste the money, and, of course, I felt perfectly safe." She shakes her head. "It's not a new story; it happens all the time in my country, but you never expect it to happen to you." She pauses now, and I see her dark eyes glistening.

"Were you attacked?" I ask.

She nods with tears streaking down her smooth brown cheeks. "Two men caught me from behind. I thought they were just going to rob me, and I actually let go of my purse, hoping they'd take it and run—and leave me alone."

"But they didn't?"

"Oh, they did eventually. But my purse was not the only thing they wanted. I pleaded with them, begging them as they dragged me from the sidewalk and into a dark, nasty building. I prayed out loud, asking God to help me." Now a little sob escapes, and she holds her face in her hands and just cries.

I can feel my own tears coming as full realization hits me. I can't believe this happened to her. I want to stand up and go over to her, to hug her and tell her how sorry I am, how sad this is, but I'm afraid I'll tip the canoe. "You must've been so scared," I say in a voice that sounds very small, like a child's.

She nods. "Terrified."

Then there's a long, quiet pause, and I feel it's up to me to help her to finish her terrible story. "Did they rape you, Lydia?"

She nods again, very slowly. "Yes."

"I'm so sorry, Lydia. That's…that's so wrong. *It makes me so angry…and…and…*" Then I begin to cry really hard. In fact, I think I'm sobbing even louder than she is now, and it feels like something inside me is just breaking, and I can't bear to think of poor, sweet Lydia subjected to something so horrendous, so brutal, so horribly wrong. It's like I physically ache for her. I bury my face in my hands too, and then I just cry.

"Oh, Maddie," she says in a gentle tone, "please, don't keep crying like that. I didn't mean to upset you."

I look up. "I'm…I'm sorry," I say. "But I feel so sad for you. And it makes me so furious." I shake a fist in the air. "Why do men do that? It just makes me want to go out and kill someone."

"I know. Believe me, I've been through all the emotions. Denial

and disbelief, then a deep, dark depression, and then I got so furious
I felt like I hated everyone. I was even angry at God. I honestly didn't
know if I'd ever get over it. And I wanted to kill myself too."

"What did you do?"

"I had to return to God," she says.

"But you were angry at him?"

She shakes her head and wipes her wet cheeks with the palms of
her hands. "I had to step away from my anger, Maddie. I knew if I
continued being mad at God I would be left with nothing—I might
as well be dead."

"Yeah, I guess I sort of understand."

"And, surprisingly, after going through all that, all those turbulent
emotions and everything, and after I returned to God and put my life
in his hands, I actually wanted to live. I mean I really *wanted* to live.
Before all that happened, well, I guess I took things for granted, and
I wasn't even sure what I wanted to do with my life."

There's a long silence now, just the sound of birds and the breeze
in the trees and the water lapping the sides of the canoe. But I can tell
that she has something more to say. So I sit there, almost holding my
breath as I wait for her to continue.

"There's something else," she says in a quiet voice, "something I
want you to know, something that I have kept very private." She takes
a deep breath. "As a result of that night, of being raped, I have HIV."

Somehow I knew this was coming, but even so, I feel as if I've
been punched in the stomach. This is so wrong.

"I didn't get tested, not right at first. Like so many others who live
in fear, I didn't want to know. But then I got really scared about dying,

and I forced myself to go in and be tested. Of course, it was positive. That's when I felt like my life was over—my dreams were gone."

"I'm so sorry."

"That was when I really struggled with God, trying to figure out what to do, whether or not to give up. Being raped was horrible, but HIV felt like the last straw, the thing that pushed me clear over the edge. Going down that low is what made me cry out for God. It's why I had to give in to him, to seek his way instead of my own. That's when I started going back to church, and I made a couple of really good friends. And they helped me realize that I needed to tell my parents the truth about all this." She closes her eyes. "I think that was the hardest thing I've ever done."

"Your poor parents. No wonder they're so worried."

"Yes. I always believed they loved me, but I suppose I sort of took that for granted too. And it wasn't something we ever really talked about. But I was shocked at how brokenhearted they were to find out about this. It was as if they felt it almost as much as I had. That's when I knew they really loved me."

"And that's why they're so protective of you."

"Yes. I know it makes no sense. I mean what happened *happened*, and there is no changing that. But I do understand their fears, especially Mom's."

"Yes, so do I." Now I feel guilty for judging Mrs. Johnson. No wonder she was freaking out over this trip. No wonder she's so careful for Lydia's safety.

"After they found out, they didn't want me to go back to my job in Port Moresby, but I convinced them I had to do it. So they returned with me and met my friends at church. Then they helped me find a safer place to live, very close to work and to the clinic. My dad had heard about Dr. Larson's work. So he took me to meet him, and we discovered that although he may look old, the doctor has some very innovative ideas for treating AIDS. He took me on as his personal project, and I'm getting some of the best medicines in the world. Unfortunately, they're so expensive that most people in my country can't begin to afford them. But Dr. Larson won't take no for an answer. In return I've been volunteering at the clinic, and that led to teaching the awareness classes. Sort of a trade-off."

I nod, impressed with how maturely Lydia is handling her life. "Wow."

"And I guess this is where God makes evil work for good, Maddie. Because through all this horror, I've come to care greatly about people with AIDS in our country. I have compassion now where I would've held them in judgment and contempt before. Do you know what I mean?"

"Yes, I think so."

"And it's given me the desire to go into medicine again. Oh, I wanted to be a doctor before, but I think it was only to prove myself, to show off and impress people that a young Papua New Guinean woman could accomplish something like that. Now I know I simply want to become a doctor so I can *help* people, especially those with AIDS."

"Oh, Lydia!" I feel fresh tears coming. It's like I can't stop them today. "That's so wonderful! Honestly, I don't think I've heard anything in this country that gives me as much hope as what you've just told me. It's amazing."

"Really?" She seems honestly surprised.

"Really!" I have to shake my head as I try to allow all that she's said to fully sink in. "I mean, I feel so sorry for you and what happened—it breaks my heart—but then to hear how you're handling it, how you're trusting God and wanting to put your pain to such good use. Well, it totally blows my mind. I wish everyone could hear your story, Lydia."

She nods. "I know I should get more comfortable about telling it. But it's just not easy. There is such a stigma attached to this disease. Hardly anyone else knows."

"I know about the stigma. I've seen firsthand how people react to AIDS in this country, and I've heard the horror stories. And we went to that hospital in Port Moresby—to the AIDS ward. What a mess."

"Yes! That's exactly why I want to be a doctor. I want things to change here. And I want people to get educated. That's why I do the class. I even tell my own story, but I pretend like it's someone else's. I call the woman Tibisi, my birth mother's name—just to show that *anyone* can get AIDS and that we need to stop treating sufferers like criminals."

"And it looked like you were getting through to your class. You had their full attention."

She smiles. "Yes. Sometimes I wonder if they suspect that Tibisi is really me. But I want them to take AIDS seriously. I want them to get in and get tested or to use prevention or whatever it takes to start controlling this horrible disease. That's all that matters. We need to stop the poison before our country is in complete ruins."

"Do you think it would be okay for Sid to hear your story?" I ask.

"Yes. I've already decided to tell her. And if she wants to use it for her article, I'll give her my full permission."

"She could tell your story without giving your name," I point out.

Lydia nods. "Yes, whatever is best."

Just then I see a movement out of the corner of my eye, and I turn to see what I thought was a log now sliding down into the water without much more than a ripple. "A crocodile!" I gasp at Lydia with widened eyes. I cling to the sides of the canoe. "Do you think he can tip us over?"

"Oh, I don't think he wants to do that," says Lydia in a calm tone. But just the same, she picks up her paddle, and we start moving away from that spot.

I take my paddle and try to imitate her calm, easy strokes, wondering how she can be so brave and then realizing this young woman has been through a lot. Soon we can see Kauani up ahead, and I feel myself beginning to relax.

We dock the canoe and carefully get out. As Lydia secures it to the dock, I thank her again for sharing her story with me, telling her I'm honored that she trusts me with it.

"I feel like we're related," I say as she stands up straight. Then I reach out and give her a hug. "Like we could be sisters."

She grins, then pulls away and studies my face. "Well, we don't look much alike, Maddie."

"I don't know," I say as I pull out my ponytail and set my wild curls free. "Our hair is similar."

"Yes," she laughs as she gives her shoulder length curls a shake. "It is."

"And, don't forget, our mothers are similar."

She nods. "Maybe we are related."

We find Sid sitting out on the deck that wraps around one end of the house, swatting at mosquitoes with one hand as she writes something in a notebook. "Hey, you guys," she says. "How was the lazy river?"

"Pretty cool," I say. "We scared a crocodile."

She laughs. "Right, I'll bet he was shaking in his boots. Donna and Tom went to a village down the river to check on a woman who's having a difficult childbirth. They expect to be home before dark, and I told them we'd start dinner." She glances at her watch. "She laid some stuff out and wrote down some instructions. Looks pretty straightforward to me."

"I'm surprised you didn't go with them," I say as I sit in a chair across from her. "Sounds like it could be interesting."

"I considered going, but I didn't like the idea of leaving you two young things alone in the village."

I glance over to where women are coming home in their canoes, and I hear the shrill cries of children's voices as they run and play about the village. "I don't really think we'd be alone," I point out.

"You know what I mean."

I glance at Lydia now, wondering if this might be a good time for her to tell Sid her story. I can tell by her eyes she's thinking the same thing. I sort of nod, hoping she'll take it as a hint.

"I just told Maddie something out there," she begins, "something that might be useful for your article, Sid."

I nod eagerly. "It'll be hugely useful, Sid. It's an amazing story."

Sid leans forward with interest, patting the chair beside her. "Come and tell me, Lydia. I've got the article mostly outlined, but it still seems a little flat to me. The poison metaphor is helpful, but something seems to be lacking. Maybe you've got the missing link."

"I think she does," I say, standing. "And since I've already heard the story, maybe I should go start dinner."

"Thanks, sweetie," says Sid.

From inside the house, I can hear their voices, mostly Lydia's, as I read the instructions, then cut up the vegetables that Donna's laid out in the kitchen. I pray as I quietly work, asking God to help Lydia with the telling of her story as well as with her continued healing, and then I ask God to help my aunt put Lydia's words to good use. Somehow I know this will be the case. Somehow I know that's why we came to this country.

But I believe there's more to it. I think our trip has as much to do with becoming friends with Lydia as it does Sid's article. And I'm so thankful God was orchestrating the whole trip. Mostly, I'm just amazed.

TWENTY

After a few more pleasant days in Kauani, we head back down the river with Micah in the motorboat and then fly out of Wewak and back to the highlands on Friday. Peter meets us at the Aiyura airstrip in the Land Rover, and we reach Lydia's village just before dark.

After hearing Lydia's amazingly moving story, Sid and I decided to take her parents up on their invitation to return for the dedication ceremony on Saturday. Tom radioed Mr. Johnson ahead of time to let them know we were coming, and they seem genuinely happy to see us when we arrive at dinnertime. Or perhaps they're just relieved that we've delivered their daughter back to them safe and sound.

Our little plan is to discuss Lydia's future with them after dinner. Of course, Lydia is unaware of this. Sid and I barely put this plan together the night before we left Kauani, whispering in the dark after we were sure everyone was asleep. After a few fairly expensive long-distance phone conversations with John while we were in Wewak, Sid is now certain that Lydia's college expenses will be completely covered by several wealthy and generous sponsors. And she can't wait to tell the Johnsons the good news. The question is, how will they receive it?

Finally the dinner dishes are cleaned up and put away, and Sid announces she'd like to talk to Lydia's parents about something important. We sit down together at their dining table with a pot of black tea and a plate of lemon squares that Mrs. Johnson made for dessert. The room is quiet, and I can feel the expectation in the air.

Sid clears her throat, then begins. "I don't want to overstep any boundaries here, but I'd like to tell you something I think is very exciting."

It's clear by their expressions that she has their undivided attention, so she continues. "When we first met Lydia in Port Moresby, we were so impressed with her spirit and her compassion for AIDS victims that we wanted to do something to help with her continued education. We know she's working to earn college money, but she's such a bright and dedicated girl that it seems a shame to delay her education, and we—"

"But what if Lydia isn't *ready* to continue her education?" interrupts her mother. "Perhaps she has delayed going to school for a reason." She glances at Lydia, but Lydia's expression is unreadable.

"I understand your concern for Lydia," says Sid in a gentle tone. "I admit I didn't understand it the last time I brought this subject up. To be perfectly honest, I thought you were being overly controlling and not taking her feelings into full account. But now I know why you feel so protective of her, and if I were her mother, I'm sure I'd feel just the same."

Mrs. Johnson blinks as if she's shocked.

"I told them about what happened to me," says Lydia in a quiet voice.

"But why?" exclaims Mrs. Johnson. "I thought you wanted to keep this matter private."

"I felt like it was something I needed to do, Mom. And I knew I could trust them."

"And Lydia *can* trust us," Sid assures her mother. "Of course, I'd love to use her story in my article, with a pseudonym to protect her privacy. I think the impact of her personal experience will help more people understand the devastating effect of the disease in this country and why it's so vital that people open their eyes, not to mention their hearts."

"That makes sense to me," says her dad.

Mrs. Johnson nods sadly. "Yes, I suppose it does. That is, if Lydia is comfortable with it."

"I am," says Lydia. Then she turns to Sid. "But I'm still amazed at your offer to help with my schooling. And, if my parents agree, I'd love to take you up on it. More than anything, I want to go back and finish my schooling. I want to specialize in immune-deficiency diseases; I want to make a difference in my country. More now than ever."

"To be honest," says Mrs. Johnson, "part of our initial hesitation in regard to your help with Lydia's tuition was because I was afraid you'd change your mind when you found out the truth."

"The *truth?*" Sid frowns, and I can tell she's not comfortable with Mrs. Johnson's attitude regarding AIDS.

"I mean that she has, you know, the AIDS virus." Mrs. Johnson looks very uneasy now. "It sounds terrible, and it's not the way I see it, but some people might think sending a girl with AIDS through college, well, wouldn't be a very good investment."

"Well, we think it's a *fantastic* investment," says Sid, smiling directly at Lydia. "I've never met anyone as brave as your daughter." She looks at Mr. and Mrs. Johnson. "You should be very proud."

They both smile. "We are," says her dad as he puts his hand over his wife's.

"And I think she's going to make a fantastic doctor," I say. "I've already seen her interacting with patients, and I can tell she has a gift."

"We can go over the details later," says Sid, "but be assured, my editor has been talking to some of his friends, as well as his church, and even some of the people back at the magazine, and this is something everyone is supporting."

"This is so exciting," says Mrs. Johnson, taking Lydia's hand in hers. "I mean, if it is what you really want to do."

"It is!" Lydia's eyes are bright and hopeful. "More than anything, that's what I want!"

We talk until it's late, trying to decide which medical school would be best to apply to and when Lydia should start. Sid promises to put her assistant onto finding the best HIV treatments available in the United States. Then Mr. Johnson reminds us that tomorrow will be a busy day with the dedication of the New Testament, and we all head off to bed.

The Bible dedication is a huge success, attended not only by the Lomokako tribe but some neighboring tribes as well. There are speeches and songs and more speeches and more songs, followed by what they call a *mumu*. This is a New Guinean–style barbecue with a whole hog cooked on hot rocks in a pit beneath the ground, along with a lot of local vegetables and fruits that are truly delicious. Anyway, the party goes on and on, and by the time it's over, everyone seems genuinely happy to have their New Testaments in tok ples.

On Monday morning we fly back to Port Moresby with Lydia. Our flight out of the country looks like a tight connection, but fortunately (and typically), it's running late, which allows us a few more minutes to tell Lydia good-bye. We hug and cry in the airport terminal, and it honestly feels like I'm leaving a family member behind.

"You've got my e-mail address and phone number and fax number?" Lydia asks me, although I'm sure she knows I do.

"Yes," I assure her. "And I'll fax the community-college schedule to you as soon as I get home. Just in case there are some classes you haven't taken yet."

"Wouldn't that be amazing," she says, "if we got to go to school together?"

"It would be awesome," I tell her. "I would totally love it. I just hope they have some classes you still need."

"And that they've got an opening."

I wave my hand. "I'm sure they do."

"Then you could both transfer to the University of Washington for winter or spring semester," says Sid. "As I told your parents, Lydia, I've heard their med school is outstanding, but I'll send you all the information."

"And I'll check out their Web site," says Lydia.

"This could be so cool," I tell Lydia. "I know my parents would totally love you. And you could have Jake's room. Most of his stuff is out of it anyway."

"I'll be praying that God opens the right doors," says Lydia.

"Me too," I say as I hug her again.

Then it's time for the plane to load, and we wave good-bye and climb aboard our Air Niugini flight headed back to Australia.

"I was checking e-mail in the airport," says Sid in a slightly mysterious tone, "while you and Lydia were getting those fruity drinks."

"And?"

"And your friend Ryan wants to know what happened to you."

"Huh?"

"He e-mailed me to ask why he hasn't heard from you since we left. He sounded really concerned, and I can tell he's worried that something is wrong between the two of you."

"But I e-mailed him a lot," I point out.

Then Sid asks me who my server is, and I tell her. "That could be the problem," she says. "They're not terribly reliable, Maddie."

"So Ryan was really worried?" I say hopefully, not even admitting I'd been worrying about him too, worrying that he had forgotten all about me.

"Yep. I think that boy is into you, Maddie."

I smile and lean back in my seat. "Cool."

Sid sighs and leans back too. "Wow, I can't believe we've only been gone a couple of weeks. What a trip this has been."

"You can say that again."

"So you're not sorry you came?"

"Are you kidding? I'm sorry we have to leave."

"It was different from Ireland, wasn't it?"

I laugh. "Well, they're *both* islands, and they're *both* green, but that's about where the similarities end. And, you know, I really loved Ireland, but I think this trip was even better."

She smiles. "Well, I think I'll keep you on as my assistant. You certainly earned your keep."

"Cool." I glance at her. "So do you have some other big trip planned already?"

She just shakes her head. "Actually, I wouldn't mind a *real* vacation. I've been working steadily all summer, and this New Guinea trip took a lot out of me. I'm feeling pretty worn out. What I wouldn't give just to stretch out on a nice quiet beach somewhere—I mean a *safe* beach."

"Do we get to stay in Hawaii on the way home?" I ask hopefully.

She frowns. "I wish."

Then she pulls a slightly wrinkled travel brochure from a pocket in her briefcase. "My friend Barb gave me this right before I left. She said I should check it out."

"Cabo San Lucas?" I read. "Where's that?"

"On the tip of Baja, Mexico." She smiles. "They say the beaches down there are delightful, and you can get a great big, padded lounge chair where the cabana boys bring you frosty fruity drinks with little umbrellas sticking out."

"Need any company?"

She laughs. "*Sí, sí, señorita.* But of course!"

About the Author

MELODY CARLSON is the award-winning author of more than one hundred books for adults, children, and teens. She is the mother of two grown sons and lives near the Cascade Mountains in central Oregon with her husband and a chocolate Lab retriever. She is a full-time writer and an avid gardener, biker, skier, and hiker.